THE

MW00776827

The Inheritance
of a
Swamp Witch

Sonia Taylor Brock

DEDICATION

This book is dedicated to

the memory of

my Sister, Jamie

and my

Grandmother (MaMaw).

May they Rest in Peace

You will live on forever in our Memories

Also with deep appreciation for my husband James who wouldn't let me quit and a special thanks to Troy Endres who volunteered to be my guinea pig and gave me the Weapons and Tactics advice that helped pull the book together.

CONTENTS

1 DAN'S JOURNAL - PREFACE

My name is Dan Rawlings, I am an Investigative Journalist. I have been assigned the daunting task of telling a story that no one in their right mind would ever believe was fact and not fiction. Hell, I don't believe it myself. However, I know it is true because I was there.

These are my observations and experiences as they happened. I would like to say, to the best of my knowledge that I was not under the influence of any narcotic or hallucinogen at the time or presently.

As a side note, you will understand, as you read this story, why even *I* might have some reservations about my sobriety. I have asked that question and have been assured that my experiences were definitely not chemically induced and that my sanity is intact.

Not quite certain how to begin this story, I will do my best and start with things chronologically so as not to confuse you. I have attempted to convey to you, the reader, the places, personalities, historical and literary references and dialects that were involved and in some cases conducted a little research with my newfound "Insight" to be able to fill in the blanks, so that you may come to the same conclusion that I have. I *have* become quite blissfully insane. It *must* be, because at the risk of sounding like and old Sci-Fi movie, any other explanation would alter our entire perception of the world as we know it.

2 THE ACCIDENT

From Official Louisiana State Highway Patrol Accident Report: Jamie Delahousse was driving Southwest on Hwy 90 during a heavy thunderstorm. Passing over a bridge, the car hydroplaned and she lost control of the vehicle, she hit the guardrail and the car went over the bridge plunging them down into the bayou below.

The driver of a car that was traveling some distance behind saw the accident and he pulled over and ran down the embankment to find the car nose down in the raging water. Unable to reach the mother, the man heard the strangled cries of two children that had been thrown into the back window of the car by the impact.

One of the children was grasping the other infant who was no more than two or three months old, both little girls.

The driver grabbed the children and waded back to the bank with them. When he set them down and turned to go back for the mother, the car was swept away in the raging current. The vehicle was never recovered.

Department of Social Services
Case File 566009
Foster Parent Release Interview
June 20, 1969
Amy Thibodeaux – Case Worker
Madeline Delahousse age -Female
Adelaide Delahousse age –Female

Raised by foster parents Henrietta and Gerard Broussard, the children spent their first three years waiting for a family member to come in search of them. No one ever came forward.

The girls clung to each other and would scream incessantly when separated in the beginning, but when they were together they were calm and docile. Both children would only communicate with each other in something resembling a phenomenon called "Twin-Speak".

It consisted of a musical gibberish with chirps, humming, occasional grunts and a strange throat warble that almost sounded like purring. Doctors were baffled by their strange behavior citing that it was the result of a shock-induced psychosis resulting in a type of mental retardation.

Although characterized as mentally impaired by the State of Louisiana, the girls were obedient and would follow instructions. However, they seemed to understand everything that was being said to them, but refused to respond verbally to others.

The oldest child led the youngest in everything. They learned very quickly but were mischievous as they developed. They would hide in strange places to be alone together. When trying to coax them out of their hiding places, they were prone to biting and scratching, growling and hissing if you tried to force them out. They loved chocolate and other treats, so bribing them out into the open proved to be more successful than anything. The foster parents, at their wits end named them "The Little Wild Ones".

The oldest child preferred puzzles and mechanical toys to play with while the youngest preferred dolls, stuffed animals and sparkly things. They had an abundance of energy and ravenous appetites and would eat just about anything. Foods high in sugar made them act as if they were sedated. The girls were never sick, not even a runny nose.

When they were infants, their appearance was striking in that they showed certain characteristics common to Down-Syndrome children. Upturned, almond shaped eyes, small hands and feet. However, their fingers, toes and limbs were long and slender, almost graceful. As they grew older and their features grew more defined, they looked like little mythical Pixies.

Another odd feature was their coloring. Both girls had pale almost translucent skin and extremely vibrant eye color. The oldest girl had electric blue eyes and the youngest child's eyes were the iridescent green and gold of an Ammolite Gemstone.

When the girls focused their attention on you their pupils would dilate to wide open and it was as if you were being pinned to the spot by a predator and were being evaluated as a predator evaluates whether or not he is threatened, hungry or just not interested. A slow blink and a smile always followed the stare releasing you from its hold and suddenly it would occur to you that that you had been holding your breath.

Separately, they maintained an aloof demeanor but would tolerate being held and cuddled as long as they were in the same room. They were also inquisitive of most things. They would pick something up and fiddle with it and examine it until they mastered its purpose and function and then immediately discard it without another thought.

They loved being outdoors and were constantly pushing the limits of their boundaries. Several times the police had been called because they had turned up missing. Then after a while, they would suddenly be standing behind you wondering what you were looking for, completely ignorant of the dilemma they had caused. The Broussard's eventually came to the conclusion that if they were missing, they would come back in a couple of hours.

Custody Change

When the girls were 4 and 5 years old, an old woman came to the door claiming to be their great grandmother Estelle Eschte. She said that her granddaughter, Jamie was expected back from New Orleans because her husband, Barry Delahousse had been injured on an oil rig and was taken to Oschner's Hospital in New Orleans the week before. Jamie and the girls had been visiting with him because he had been in a coma and in critical condition.

Jamie called and said that he had been stabilized but was still comatose and that she was going to have some of Barry's family who lived in Baton Rouge and were staying in a hotel watch over the babies until he got better. Her family didn't get too worried when they didn't hear from Jamie for a couple of days because calls to the hospital confirmed that Barry was still in a coma.

This went on for several weeks until Barry's sister called upset because Jamie had not been at the hospital with her husband since that first week. No one knew where she had gone.

The old woman said that she had never given up searching for her granddaughter and her babies. She said she had searched the newspapers in every town she went for any news. When asked about Jamie's parents, she said that Jamie was born out of wedlock and when Jamie was an infant her Mother, Marie, ran off with a businessman heading for California and they had never heard from her again. Mrs. Eschte took Jamie and raised her until adulthood.

Mrs. Eschte produced marriage certificates, birth certificates and all the necessary documentation to claim the girls. She found them by reading an old news-paper article about a car accident in Raceland, La., and two unidentified children. She also produced a family picture of the girls positively identifying the children with their mother.

The girls were released to Mrs. Estelle Eschte on June 17, 1969.

3 CHASING A LEAD TO THE LAND OF SWAMPS

Chasing an obscure lead on a possible heir to the Hamilton Fortune, I decided to drive to New Orleans from Los Angeles. I had the money for a plane ticket, but then I would have had to rent a car and have nothing to eat until I tracked down the records I needed.

I couldn't believe that the woman at the Public Records department could not be begged, bribed or sweet talked into making copies of the sealed documents and sending them to me for any amount of money. She babbled something about the family those records belonged to would not appreciate their business being scattered across the country without their knowledge and no amount of money would make her cross that family. If I wanted to see those records I could come and make the copies myself.

In my opinion, this is solid proof that in these backwater southern towns, the people are still living 20 or so years behind the rest of us. They act like they have never heard of such things as email, faxes and copiers for God's sakes. This fine example of 'Southern Hospitality' was going to make me have to risk everything I had on this story. If my hunch panned out though, this would be the story of the century and help me make a name for myself so that I could do more than free-lance reporting for a couple of celebrity gossip rags from which I had until recently earned my meager living.

Initial Notes – 3/5/2011   *Billionaire Webster Hamilton died back in the 70's leaving a widow Marie Hamilton. Marie died 3 months ago a childless widow. The will left everything to a "charitable organization", the Our Lady of the Lake Foundation. They worked with special children. Webster's niece and nephew, Henrietta and William Hamilton, were contesting the will.*

The drama that ensued has made national headlines. The Niece and Nephew had launched an investigation into what the foundation was all about and found out that it was simply a research foundation looking into children with E.S.P. and other abilities. The tabloids touted HOAX as loud as they could to fight the decision of the will. But when pressed, Webster's Lawyers said that not only had Webster made the will long before he experienced the dementia of old age, but that the will was made as part of one of the first iron clad prenuptial contracts ever recorded. Apparently, Marie insisted that a set fee be sent to the foundation every month that they were married and that the entire estate would be handed over upon their deaths. Our Lady of the Lake foundation was headquartered in Baton Rouge, Louisiana where Marie was supposedly from.

Doing a little poking around, I found out that Marie's birth certificate stated that it was an official copy from the hall of records in Baton Rouge, but she was actually born and raised in Houma, Louisiana. When I called and questioned the records clerk in Houma, she said that yes, Ms. Marie was born in Houma, but she couldn't tell whether her child was alive or dead.

Jackpot! If Marie had a child and I could produce evidence and be the first to break the story, it would change my career! No one would ever make fun of the way I dress again! (My editor said my hats made me look like Carl Kolchak.) Hey, what can I say, direct sunlight hurts my purty blues. I've been sensitive since I was a kid. For some reason, sunglasses made me feel like I was in a cage looking out. Baseball caps make my head sweat. I have thick hair now, but I have heard that baseball hats make you go bald early.

My first stop would be the Houma Daily Courier Newspaper. Although they still kept all records from 1990 – back on microfiche, anything from 1990 forward was on computer files. What I needed would naturally be on microfiche, the same as what the clerk at the Courthouse Records office told me.

The courthouse would have just the records, but the newspaper would have information. I knew that it would take some time to track down any birth announcements and I was hoping that my Los Angeles Press Pass would open more doors and loosen some tongues and get me a helping hand or two to make this go a little faster.

I was tired and starving by the time I got to Houma having made the drive straight through with only a couple hours of shut eye and coffee with Red Bull Chasers. A flat tire in Texas had me limping in on the little donut and kept my speed down to 55 without the steering becoming too erratic.

The heat and humidity were absolutely oppressive clinging to me like a hot wet blanket. I pulled into a café on the edge of town called Benoit's. Everything on the menu was foreign to me. The only thing I could find that was remotely familiar was a Po Boy. If my memory was correct, that was something like a sub sandwich.

The waitress came up to me and said "What's ya pleasure, Chere?" Obviously confused at her accent, I just stared at the menu for a minute trying to figure out what she was asking me when she smiled and said "You from outta town?" "Yeah" I said, "What do you put on a Poy Boy?" She laughed and said "Arrybody's got der own recipes, yeah, but we done outta French Bread ride naw, but we make de bes Mufalotta's in Loosiana."

Still trying to understand her, I said "Ooookaaay, what's in it?' Again she made a deep throaty laugh and asked "You 'lergic to seafood, Chere?" I shook my head negatively and she said "Den Ahl fix you one mahsef an if ya don' lahk it, ya don' pay". Well, if I translated correctly, that would fit right into my budget of almost broke.

She walked away and a busboy came and put 3 small dishes of sauces on the table with a beer and a basket of what looked like little dried shrimp? The busboy pointed to the basket and said, "Ya eat dem lahk peanuts." Then he pointed to the sauces and said "Remolawd, Tabasco, and Peppa Vinegar."

Tentatively, I put a couple of the shrimp in my mouth and an explosion of chewy, tender fresh sea and shrimp and salt surprised me. They were good, and the remoulade was the best of the sauces with a spicy creaminess that offset the salt in the shrimp, and apparently they were addictive. Before I knew it, the shrimp, sauces and my beer were gone.

Now my mouth was watering in anticipation of the Muffelata. The waitress came up a few minutes later with a baked sandwich the size of a deep-dish pie and a fresh beer. I picked up one half of the sandwich and had to stretch my mouth as far as it would go to get a bite. Cheeses, garlic, seafood, olives and some kind of fruit, combined with a toasted, rough, buttery texture. Oh. My. God! I almost cried. The waitress smiled again and said "Eight dollas, Chere." I slapped a 20 on the table. It was worth it. Besides, there was enough here for two meals or more.

Completely satiated, 45 minutes and three beers later with a brown paper bag holding more dried shrimp for later, directions to the nearest motel, and a basic guide to the city, I had accomplished more than I would have in a half a day on my own. I was also assured that Coffee and Beniet's were available at 6:00am, as the café was open 24 hours and seemed to be a busy local hangout.

4 DOWN AND DIRTY DETECTIVE WORK

The only thing my Press Pass got me was a 'help yourself' to the coffee pot in the break-room. The Houma Daily Courier archives were just as expected and typical of most small town newspapers. Settling down, I began searching the year that Marie was born. 1920 was a busy time back then.

Births were not acknowledged In the papcr unless you were wealthy or of some prominence in the community. The paper consisted of about 10 pages and it was called *Le Courrier de Houma*. One half of it was in French and the other half was in English.

Prohibition and Women's right to vote were the political topics of the day and the rest of the news consisted of any major or minor crimes, recipes, some small hand-drawn advertising, and Mardi Gras announcements and local society gossip.

I would have to expand my search to span the 1919 – 1930 timelines. Marie was apparently a very common female French name. I had scanned another 7 years when I found something else. An article about Mardi Gras stated that the princesses had been named for the Krewe of the Houmas. They included the name Marie Evangeline Eschte and that her parents were named Estelle and Claude Eschte. AH HA!!! It fit!!!

Armed with a certified copy of the birth certificate (even though the mother's name is not legible) and these news articles, I had a family name to search on and I was building on the background that would support my expose!

I was in good spirits in spite of the clanging and banging the janitor had done while I conducted my searches. The warty, hunch backed little man almost seemed to be snooping into what I was doing. Every time I would look up, he was behind me looking over my shoulder. It was a small town after all and they probably didn't get many out-of-towner's looking through the archives unless they were residents looking for family tree kind of stuff.

It was after 3:00pm and I didn't have time to get to the County Courthouse. Oh, excuuuse me, the clerk snottily corrected me when I called; "We don't have counties we have Parishes". So, I decided to dig a little more.

I found another article dated August 4, 1942 from a police report about a young girl, M. Eschte, who had been assaulted. Apparently, a family member heard her screams and came to her rescue and must have frightened her attacker away. No positive identification was made on the perpetrator and he was never caught. The girl had been sent to the hospital but was later released to her family.

Another article appeared about 10 months later of a newborn that was found in a basket on the front steps of Terrebonne Hospital and was now a ward of the state until the mother could be identified. Coincidence? What was with these people anyway? Children were being born all over the place and the parents turned up missing or dead. Strange, to say the least.

It got me to wondering why would they do that, and it occurred to me that back then, having a child out of wedlock would not only make the child a pariah, but then family would also bear the brunt of the stigma associated with having a bastard in the family. Hmmm….. scandals that went back two, maybe three generations….this was getting better and better. In my experience, everyone had skeletons in their closet but this family had a warehouse! I had to get documentation! But it was now 5:30 and I was being shooed out because they were closing down for the night crew. No public allowed.

It looked like I might get more information by looking for family names than birth records. Where is the best place to find out about a family other than birth records? Why death records of course. Where do you find death records other than obituaries?…. Cemeteries and funeral homes of course, of course!

I would have to make a trip to the local library and hopefully they would have something on local families with some computer access. Having to pawn my laptop for this trip was sucking big time. Press Passes didn't get you special favors with the libraries here either. They ran the place like Fort Knox! Library cards for non-residents were $15.00! At this rate, I was going to max out my credit cards in no time.

To top it off, this time I had to share a table with another man and woman who stank and argued the entire time. They wouldn't leave no matter how many shushes and dirty looks I gave them. I could barely concentrate. I changed tables once and the woman got even more agitated with the man and came over to my table to sit and make her point in the argument. I know it's a public place and all, but couldn't they go to a park or something?

What was interesting is that in this area, graves were mostly family crypts. Because of the sea level, you couldn't dig more than 4 feet without hitting water. Crypts usually were bought by a family and passed down from generation to generation.

On the event of a new death, the crypt was cleaned and old coffins were rotated out when the bodies had dis-integrated. Due to the rapid rate of decay from the heat and moisture this process could take as little as one year. The ashes of the deceased were collected and kept in burial urns on shelves within the crypt. However, a list of each deceased was placed on the outside of the crypt by means of a stone plaque that was added when they died just like small individual tombstones. Voila! A family tree!

A listing of local cemeteries was indeed available. I made a couple of calls to the cemeteries and found out that I would have to come in person to get individual names of each deceased. I had to be a court official to obtain printed information even though it was a matter of public record. Apparently, Eschte was a common last name as well.

At 7:30pm, my stomach was grumbling and I was back at Benoit's. Donna, my waitress laughed and said "Ah tol' you ya'd be back". This time, I sat at the counter and surveyed the place a little better while I ate some more dried shrimp. Louisiana's answer to Chips and Salsa? Bernice went to get me some gumbo 'to make me smack my mama'.

I noticed the central tables were picnic-style covered in several layers of brown paper. Booths lined the wall of windows and counter and extended the length of the other wall. It reminded me of a rustic 50's diner. The place was clean but well-worn and the customers talked to each other like men in the barbershop on the Andy Griffith Show. I felt like I needed to look out for Aunt Bea to come in.

A businessman, a cop and a couple of locals and me were at the counter while two families sat at the picnic tables with a couple obviously on a date occupying a booth.

The Busboy, "Tee Boy" was sweeping the floor when the cook came out lugging a huge aluminum pot. Tee Boy ran over to help the cook carry the pot over to the table of one of the families and then they proceeded to dump the whole pot right into the middle of the table. Now I understood why there were rolls of paper towels and brown paper covering the tables.

The smell was fantastic. The pot had contained small lobster-like bright red crustaceans (I learned later were crawfish not crayfish) with an assortment of whole cooked potatoes, corn on the cob, peppers, whole onions and other goodies. While I was looking, I watched everyone dig in with his or her hands. They would pick one up, break the tail off and begin sucking on the heads! YEUCK!! Shells and heads began hitting buckets sitting on the floor like rain.

The cook came over and flopped onto the stool next to me. He mopped his brow with a rag and adjusted the bandana he used as a sweatband on his forehead and lit a cigarette. Apparently smoking in public was still allowed here.

The man leaned over to me and said with that deep musical tone they all seemed to have "Mah cuzin, he say to me, "I done suck no heads, no... but I eat da hell outta some tail, yeah" He chuckled, extended his hand and introduced himself; "Lucky Benoit. You gonna be 'roun here awhile?"

I shook his hand and said "I don't know, I came here to do some research on one of the local families here. I'm kind of a history buff, but I'm having a little trouble getting information." He said "Yep 'sa lotta history here. Who ya looking up?" He obviously didn't buy the history buff bit, but I replied, "A family, and I'm not sure how to pronounce it correctly….. E S C H T E?"

"Dat would be Esh tay" Dere's alotta dem roun here, yeah. Which one ya aimin fuh?" I said "Marie Eschte" and the cop at the end of the counter coughed and looked my way.

Lucky turned to him and said "Hey, Joe, zat name sound familiar to you?" The cop sat up and said "Not too sure, But Ah can do a lil poking 'roun and mebbe ask MaMere if she knows."

He gave Lucky a pointed look and Lucky turned back to me and asked why I was looking up the Eschte's. I tried to act like I hadn't noticed the hidden look or the sudden tension in the room. I had a feeling that telling them I was a reporter working on a story to uncover a scandal wouldn't earn me any brownie points.

I looked at the cop and said that a long lost relative had passed away and there was some question about a substantial inheritance involved.

Lucky said "No, dat name done ring no bells." The cop said, "Yeah, I'll check wit MaMere, she knows everybody's bidnez. She knows all da Eschte's this side of the Mississippi to Texas. Whar's dis relative stay at?" I looked at him "Stay? ….. Oh, you mean live?" "Yeah, whar dey from?"

I was having a hard time with the dialect. I first thought that it was from being uneducated and then I realized that the cop was clearly educated and came to the conclusion that it was part of their culture. I replied "From California, Los Angeles specifically." The cop said again that the name didn't sound familiar and he didn't know of any Eschte's from there.

Donna came up and sat the bowl of Gumbo down and said, "You eat dat an ya on ya way to bein a firs class coon-ass transplant." The cop got up from his meal and started toward the door and then turned and asked, "What'd ya say ya name was?"

I looked at him and smiled, knowing I hadn't told him or anyone what my name was yet. I said Dan Rawlings. Now I knew when he checked me out all that he would find is that I'm a free-lance writer. For once, my not being on the payroll as an employee would work to my advantage. Hell, even my Press Pass wasn't mine; it was still on loan from the photographer at my paper who paid me to stand in the press line until he could get there. Let the cop look. Then he said "You at da Motel 6, yeah?   If Ah find anyting, Ah'll let ya know".   He had already looked. He was not only educated, but he was smarter than he appeared. This could get tricky.

5 TOO MANY QUESTIONS

Lucky and Donna watched Dan walk out of the Diner. She leaned over to him and said "He seems like a nice man." Lucky nodded and said "Yeah, but he's askin a lotta questions about Ms. Marie. Dat ain't a good sign, non." He looked at her and asked if she could sense anything odd about the man.

She said that she had touched him on the shoulder and tried to get a reading and her hand started to get hot. She thought it might just be that the man just normally ran hot, so she told Tee Boy to brush up against him and see if he felt the same thing. Tee Boy didn't sense anything unusual and said he felt pretty normal to him.

Lucky thought about what she said and then asked her if her hand got hot as soon as she touched him or when she tried to sense something. She did think about it and said, "You're raht Chere. I didn't feel anyting til I started to try to get a read on 'im. My hand started to get hot like he was blocking me." Lucky nodded again and went into the back to make some phone calls.

He called Joe on his cell phone and told him what Donna reported feeling. Joe asked Lucky if the man said where he was going and who he had been talking to. Lucky told him that Donna had been friendly with him and given him directions to the courthouse, the library and the cemetery.

Lucky chuckled and said "Ya gotta hand it to him man, dat was a good idea he had yeah...Going to de Cemetary is de best way ta find out family business roun' here. We done had too many floods and hurricanes for many paper records to survive and be able to give much information about anybody... unless he got real lucky and could read between the de lines of what

29

der is. Raht now de man don' even know what he's lookin fuh."

Joe finished the phone call with a caution for Lucky to keep watching the man. Joe called Cecile to ask her if she had seen MaMere pass that way recently. She told him that she had seen MaMere in her pirogue coming down the bayou this morning. Joe didn't think it was all that odd that MaMere would be traveling alone she came to town from time to time by herself. However, she hadn't taken her pirogue out in quite a while. He always thought it was funny nobody ever noticed that the damn pirogue didn't even have a motor.

Joe made some more calls to the Library and talked with the young Librarian there and asked if the man had been in there. She told him that he had indeed been there yesterday. Joe asked her if she could remember what research materials he used and if he said anything to her specifically. She said that if he wanted, she still had everything out that he looked up and she could show him the microfiche he got copies made of. Joe agreed to go to the library later and pick up the materials and do a little digging of his own.

Joe also made a call to the courthouse and asked for his friend in the Records Room, Amy Domingue. Amy has had a crush on him since he arrested her teenage brother for stealing Mr. Fontenot's crab traps ten years ago. She was so excited that he called for her, he had to wait a minute for her to calm down before he could ask her any questions.

Finally, Amy told him that the man had not been in yet, but that she could find a way to delay him if he needed her to do something like that. Joe thought that might work until he could find out more about this guy. Amy was overjoyed to be able to help and he had to tell her that it would have to be something subtle and not give away the fact that they were trying to stall him in any way. She said she knew just what to do.

Joe then looked up his records in the police database and found that he was a free-lance journalist from Los Angeles. The guy was squeaky clean, no arrests, not even a parking ticket. With a little more snooping around, he found that Mr. Rawlings was not doing research for the family as he said, but that was not an investigator for the family he was searching for. He was a reporter trying to get a scoop. This was not good, not good at all.

Joe found MaMere at the farmer's Market on Grand Calliou road examining the vegetables. As he walked up to her from behind, she called to him without even turning around; "Nice day for a little shoppin, Chere. You here to give ya old MaMere some sugar and help her wit her bags."

Joe walked up and gave the old woman a hug and a kiss on the cheek. He took her bags and walked with her while she continued to look at the vegetables. He asked "What brings ya ta town on dis fine day pretty lady?" She smiled and said, "I done went over to dat young Theriot couple's house to pay dem anothah visit. Dis tahm de young Missus let me in real nice lahk. I guess she done learnt her lesson 'bout bein hospitable to a pillar of de community lahk mysef." The old woman chortled.

She continued, "When her husband stopped getting any shrimp in dey nets for a couple a weeks and she got dat awful skin rash on de same hand dat locked de door on me, she mighta got de message, yeah. You know I was jest payin my respects since dey moved in all, lahk a good neighbor should. Dey didn' even know dey was expecting tree new little bebe's before Ah came to visit. Can you believe a ting lahk dat, Chere? Dat poor young man is gonna have to git himself anothuh job on top of de shrimpin he does wit his cousin now to pay for dem new babies. He ain't gonna have much tahm fo makin anymore babies fo a long tahm too."

Joe told her that if she wanted to go "visitin" he would be happy to escort her and explain that it might be in their best interest not to close your door to Ms. Eschte if you wanted to keep getting shrimp in your nets and enjoy your pretty young wife for a while longer.

She smiled again at him and said, "You turned out ta be such a fine boy, Joe. Yer Daddy has a right to be proud." Joe a little surprised, asked "Did he say something to you."

She stopped walking for a minute and told him "Hawk, him, he's always proud of his chirren. Always's goin on about how good you all is doing. It's not good to say all dose kine a tings all de time to yer chirren, non. Dey git de big head and git all uppity if ya do dat."

Joe told her that he always thought that his Dad was disappointed in him because he didn't become a doctor or lawyer with his education. She said "Son, yer Daddy is proud of you no matter what ya do. You don' know the worry he had jest trying to keep his babies alive tru ya birthing and then ya raising. Now dat ya'll is all grown, he can relax a little, dat's all it is."

Joe smiled to himself feeling more comforted that he would like to admit, even to himself. MaMere didn't give you compliments and she didn't lie. She always knew just what to say to make him feel better.

He asked again what else brought her to town and she again said she was doing a little shopping and added that she might visit a few more friends while she was here. He asked her if she wanted him to go back with her when she was ready to leave. She told him that it wouldn't be necessary, Jean had brought her in and he would be waiting for her to take her back to her house, but later, she might have him bring a friend of hers for a visit if he didn't mind.

He told her that there was a man in town, a reporter and he was asking questions about Aunt Marie. MaMere's demeanor never changed, but she said "I know, Chere. Ah been expectin him dat's de friend Ah was tellin you bout. If Ah miss him in town, would you be a darling and fetch him to me tamorrah?"

Now this really had him reeling. He was the mysterious friend of hers. He knew the man had never heard of her but she knew him. She knew he was coming and knew what he wanted and that was ok? The whole family has always been on alert for anyone asking about Jamie or Aunt Marie. Why change now. This made him even more curious, because she wasn't answering his questions about the reporter. Just the same old riddle talk she always used when she didn't want to tell you something.

6 I COULD HAVE SWORN HER EYES TWINKLED

I got to the Parish Courthouse and found the records room and was told that yes, the computerized archives were available, but that the actual bound archives room was closed to the public today. The clerk said that the cleaning crew came in this morning and spilled a bucket of ammonia on the floor.

She explained that there is no ventilation in that room and the fumes were still too toxic to allow the public to enter. I asked her when that might be possible and she said later this afternoon they would check to see if the fumes had dissipated enough they would re-open it.

Damn, damn, and double Damn! Every time I turned around something was stopping me from getting the info I needed. I went to the computer room fuming. Maybe I would get lucky and find something like I did at the newspaper that would be useful. I inserted the access card they gave me and started scrolling names. Eschte was everywhere.

Distinguishing who was who required some knowledge of who was in each branch. These people had to be channeling rabbits... they multiplied like them.

I did find the same duplicate of Marie's birth certificate that I already had. However, on this copy, the Mother's last name was legible. I just got proof that I was on the right track at least. I still needed to find Marie's child not her mother, but this was a definite start.

Getting more and more frustrated, I was scrolling through names when an old woman came in and sat down at the terminal next to me. She was having trouble inserting the access card into the slot that gets you into the records and kept tapping the screen and the enter key.

Trying to look engrossed in what I was doing, I leaned forward a little and

pretended to be scanning a particular
record. I saw her turn to me out of the
corner of my eye, "Do ya know bout dees
tings, Chere?" and she sat there waiting for
me to answer. ARRRRGGGH! I took a
deep breath, and faced her and when I
looked into her eyes I could have sworn
her eyes twinkled at me.

Her face was as round as a pie. She
had skin the color of supple leather, but
there was still a rosy glow in her cheeks.
Silvered only on top and at her temples,
her dark hair was pulled back in a long
braid that touched the floor while she was
sitting in the chair. Softly wrinkled, it was
hard to guess her age. Her eyes were
almost a grass green. Her appearance was
of one who had had a full and happy life. I
felt like I was looking at the cover of a
National Geographic magazine of famous
figure in history. The face held wisdom
and understanding that you knew
instinctively. You just couldn't look away.

She sat there smiling and looking at me
in question. I shook my head to clear my
thoughts and asked her if she needed help.
"Jes a lil, Chere, can you find people in
dees tings" she asked tapping the
computer screen. I said sure and I began

instructing her how to insert her card on my terminal.

Then the next thing you know, I had told her who I was looking for and that it could be very important for my career if I could get the information I needed for my story. I was blabbering everything to her like a teenager on a cell phone.

Then she stopped me, saying that I had been very kind to an old woman who didn't understand how the young people do all these things nowadays. "Ah wish dis new batch o'chirren would learn some manners and help deys elders lahk deys s'pposed ta."

I asked her why she was here and she said that she had a large family and it was hard to keep track of and where they were. She said she comes to this place every once in a while to keep them straight in her head. She also said she hadn't been in since they started putting all the "countings" in these boxes. "Me, Ah always lookcd to dc books in the back, me."

I told her that's where I was hoping to be able to get the information from that I needed for my research, but that there was some kind of chemical spill and they weren't letting anyone in yet. She said "Ya done need nuttin in der anyways. I know all dats dere." She put a hand on my shoulder for support as she stood up.

Only then did I notice that she had a cane. It looked like an ancient staff Merlin himself would have carried. Gnarled and twisted, with intricate carvings all over it, it was clearly ancient. She didn't appear to lean on it for support, but she walked with it in her hand just the same. As she left, she said "Thank you young man, if you need something, come see Stella" tapping her chest. "Bon Chance Mon Amie" and she walked out.

7 BARNEY'S PISSED AND I'M GONNA DIE

The old woman was right. I didn't find anything and I needed more document-tation. Maybe there would be something in the cemeteries. I was going to have to stay a couple more days.

Damnit again! If I called the LA times and tried to get an advance for expenses, they would send one of their own and scoop me. If I called my editor, he would come down and scoop me. I was going to have to call my sister. I HATED calling her for money. She would give me the lecture AGAIN. Well, I guess I would have to take it one last time.

She worked 3rd shift in Sacramento and she was still sleeping. I would have to call her just before she left to go to work so she wouldn't have time to rant too long.

Benoit's opened at 6:00am. Coffee and Beniet's were indeed available. The coffee was so strong the spoon would stand up all by itself. But the Beniet's were out of this world. Something like a fried flat donut with no hole dredged in powdered sugar. You had to drink the coffee just to get the sugar down. Who needs Red Bull? I'd never sleep again.

Having made the call to Sandra, true to form, she gave me the lecture and agreed to wire the money to me on her way to work. I was waiting here for the Western Union to open. I don't know what her problem is, I have always paid her back.

Lucky laughed at me when he saw me take my first sip of the Godzilla of Caffeine they call coffee. He said "Now dat'll put har on ya chest and burn it off too!" Several other customers came in, fishermen, shrimpers, a few businessmen, but mostly blue collar workers and a contingency of old men that took up what was their booths at the windows, gossiping and reading the newspaper. They seemed to know most everyone who came in and asked about wives, relatives and children.

Maybe they might be able to give me another lead on Marie's child.

I walked over to them holding my coffee and addressed the group. "Have any of you gentlemen ever heard of any Eschte's from here?" There was a certain tense hesitation in the air and a roar of laughter. The loudest of the group said "Son, half dis town is related to an Eschte in one way or anothuh." A few more laughs from the rest of the group then he said "Tell us who ya looking fuh and mebbe we can hep, mebbe no."

I tried to act casual, "It would have been some time ago, Marie Eschte?" This time there was a much longer silence and no one was laughing. Then the old man looked at his friends and said "weellll, now let me tink. Marie, you say huh name was, yeah? Seems to me like Ah used to remember...that dere wuz a gurl by dat name, but she lef long tahm ago an no one evuh saw or heard from huh again." I looked from one old man to the other and every time I made eye contact they would look away, with the exception of Mr. Thinker who stared right into my eyes waiting for my reaction.

I was just about to ask about her child instead when Joe the Cop came in and told me "Ah've been looking fuh you Mister, MaMere wants you to come to her house. Come wit me and Ah'll take ya." There was a gentle murmur and some raised eyebrows going around at the cop's request.

I grabbed my hat and my notebook and turned to him as he waited for me. I looked at his name badge that read J. Eschte. Normally very observant, I can't believe I hadn't noticed the name before now. He knew all along whom I was looking for!

When we got to the car he said "We got all ya tings from da room ya was in and checked ya outta da motel and put ya stuff in ya trunk. By the way, didja know the lock on ya trunk's busted? Ya can get dat fixed soon as ya git home. I tied it down nice and tight so it will hold jest fine till ya git there. We had ya tire fixed too so you won't have no trouble leavin, no. Good ting ya was planning on leavin today, huh?"

I was soooooo gonna sue when I got my story sold! I looked at him over the roof of the car and said, "You knew all along who I was looking for didn't you?" He nodded, "Yep, but I hadn't heard anyone talk bout Taunt Marie in a long time. When she lef, it was a bad, bad time."

"So who is this MaMere?" He glanced at me kind of funny and said "I tawt ya'll met a'ready. MaMere is Taunt Marie's Mother and my Grandmother." Holy Shit! I hit pay dirt! Wait a minute, if Marie was 91 years old when she died, that would make her……

"Uh, huh….Ya jes did da math huh? MaMere is well over 100 and dat's why you comin to her." I sat back and tried to think. As hard as they were hiding things, this had to be one hell of a story.

We started driving down a two-lane road with swamp on one side and a bayou on the other for about 30 minutes.   That's when I thought, Uh Oh…, Barney's pissed and I'm gonna die. He's taking me out here to kill me and dump my body in these swamps, no one will ever find a thing, the perfect crime!

Then I thought, my sister knows that I'm here and she insisted on knowing why I needed the money, so she knows that I am working on a big story that has been covered up for years. I looked over at him and asked, "How far are we going? I have some money being wired to me for my expenses, so I will need to pick that up before close of business today." He said "Tha's o.k. I will make a call and tell 'em to hold it for ya."

Great, just great. Now I'm sure they were going to take me out to the swamps somewhere and kill me. I was replaying the scenes from the movie 'Southern Comfort' playing in my head.

Then suddenly the road ended and he pulled over to an area on the shoulder of the road. There was a run-down bait and beer shop on the bayou side of the road and he walked over to it. Surely he wouldn't kill me in a public place. I got out and he started walking toward the store. He yelled to the woman at the counter "Hey Cecile, you got a big plastic bag I can have?" The woman handed him a large green trash bag and walked away. He turned around and I kept thinking he's gonna chop me up and stuff my body in the bag! Then he handed the bag to me and said "Ya might want to put that funny hat and ya papers in the bag so they don't git wet."

I looked at him and said, "Why would they get wet? Where are we going?" He laughed in that deep musical tone, "Ya can't get der by car, no." He pointed to the dock that ran alongside the store and there was a metal boat with a flat bottom and a huge airplane propeller in a cage on the back of it.

We walked over to the boat and I put my hat and notes into the bag and tied a good knot in it.   We got on the boat and he tossed a life jacket to me and said "I'm a cop, remember? I've pulled too many people outta de water dead who was actin lahk de fool and got thrown off de boat and dey sank lahk a rock, yeah." I didn't tell him I wasn't worried about drowning, but having to swim with whatever else was in the water with me worried me a lot. I put the life jacket on and thought that maybe I was over-reacting just a tad.

At first it was like I was tied to the front of an airplane, but after a few minutes, I started noticing how beautiful and curious everything was. The air felt clean and soft. Finally!!, I wasn't scalding my lungs with the heated, almost liquid, hot air from town.

8 THE HOUSE ON OLD LADY LAKE

We went down a long bayou that turned and twisted for quite a way and then it opened up into the Gulf of Mexico. We crossed over two large bodies of water (Joe said over the mic in my headphones that you could see where the rivers and bayous met in the gulf because you could see where the brackish muddy water met the clearer water of the Gulf).

We then entered a swampy area that was marsh grasses and moss-strewn Cypress trees wider than the boat we were in. The trees gradually became closer together until from out of nowhere there was land and a large house that was sitting on a kind of raised platform. It had a very high sloping roofline that extended to cover a wide front porch.

Sitting on that front porch was the old lady from the computer room at the courthouse! "Stella?" I said. Joe looked a little puzzled and said, "Yes, this is Miz Estelle Eschte. Close friends call her Stella, acquaintances call her Miz Eschte, and family calls her MaMere." Hmmm...Joe, Lucky, and a couple of others at Benoit's said MaMere.

We walked up to the porch and I noticed she had a large pot of some green vegetables that looked like little goats horns. She was chopping them into a bowl between her feet. She smiled and patted the old straight back Chair beside her and said "You came jes in time to learn to make some koo bee yawh (court boullion – king's soup). It's a special treat dem city folks don' git ta taste." "While we're cookin up a storm, mebbe Ah kin help ya clear ya troubled head, yeah?"

She turned to Joe, "W'you be able to git da gurls fa me, Chere? It's time to bring 'em home for a while." Joe's face immediately showed concern. He stood up from his seat and walked over to her

"MaMere, you want me to call the family in for uuhh...dinner?"

She didn't even blink "No Chere, not today, but you can get Jace and the boys to bring me some crabs and oysters and tell ya Daddy to bring me some game, but go git the gurls and bring 'em back here firs." Joe looked hard at her for a moment, nodded his head once and turned and left.

I asked her "Do you have children?" "Mais Yeah, dey are my grandbabies and dey go to da school mos-a-da time, but Ah need 'em here for a tiny lil' spell." Then her eyes twinkled at me again! She got up and pushed the green horn things over to me and handed me her knife. "Here, you finish choppin deez okra and Ah'll go git the res-a-da trinity ready."

I looked at the knife she handed me. It had a bone handle with a wicked looking, slightly curved blade. It was definitely razor sharp because I just cut myself on it. It had the same carvings that were on her cane as there were on the hilt of the blade. Hmmm..., Interesting.

Carefully, I started slicing the okra into the bowl as she instructed and began thinking. It just dawned on me that Joe just left! What an idiot I am! Why didn't I leave with him and pick up my money-gram and come back here later when he brought the girls! It had taken almost two hours to get here. By the time he got back into town and then came back here, it would be too late to take me back again. I realized I was stuck here for the night. I hoped he wouldn't forget to make the "call to hold it for me" as he promised. Sandra would be frantic if he didn't. Shit!

Oh well, I was going to have to make the best of it. As I sat there slicing the okra, I began noticing the cool breeze that blew in steadily from the Gulf, the Spanish moss gently swaying in the trees and small insect noises, buzzing and chirping, some frogs croaking nearby and some kind of grunting sound. It was a strangely hypnotic lullaby that made me feel exhilarated and relaxed at the same time.

My imagination must have gotten the better of me because the colors around me started getting more vivid and then I saw a beautiful woman with long dark brown hair being led out of the water by two other silvery skinned nude women.

I have dreamed of this woman off and on for several months now. The afternoon light hit her turning her naked body into gold, dripping with sparkling diamonds of water. She just seemed to glow with sensuality. As always in my dreams she looked straight at me and smiled like she knew me.

Though the other two women were equally beautiful with green and brown hair, I barely noticed them for the now familiar woman I had been dreaming of. I thought to myself that the dreams were becoming more and more vivid and realistic.

The three women began walking toward me when the screen door banged shut and jolted me out of my musings. I know it's been a while since I had sex, but now I am having daydreams… I am going to have to do something about that and soon.

Stella looked down at me and nodded her head as she walked to her seat with more bowls and vegetables. I looked down and saw that my thumb was just pouring blood. I must have cut myself deeper than I thought.

Stella reached over to me and took the knife and put it in a basket beside her chair. She took a little pot of some green salve and grabbed my hand and put the salve on my thumb quicker than I could pull away. I started to protest and pull my hand back and when I realized that there was no more pain and it had stopped bleeding. Hey, that's good stuff.

While I was examining my thumb, she handed me another, much smaller knife and said "Ya not to good wit knives huh?" "No, at least not that one" I replied, "I was born and raised in Sacramento, California.

I guess you could say that I'm a city slicker. I don't really get into the outdoors stuff too much because my eyes are really sensitive to bright light. I guess that's why I became a journalist. I stayed indoors and read a lot as a kid. I go to the gym and run on a treadmill to keep my body healthy though."

She threw her head back and laughed at me "Mais, you jes need to pick a good shady place like dis to live, yeah." Come to think of it, I hadn't even put my hat back on since we got here and my eyes hadn't bothered me at all once we got into the swamp like they usually did the minute I went outside.

The grunting noise suddenly got louder and closer. It was followed by a roaring hiss sound. I jumped up and said, "What the hell was that?" (The climate here also must be affecting my muscles because I felt very stiff legged as if been sitting in that chair a long time.) She sighed and put her bowl down and grabbed her cane. She thumped the floor of the porch hard a couple of times with the end of her cane and said "Thas' jest Jean Lafitte, he gits kinda riled up when Ah have a good looking young man come ta visit. He's being a bad, bad man again, yeah."   I thought to myself that doesn't sound like a man, it sounds like some kind of animal...

Then a humungous alligator came lumbering out from under the porch hissing and roaring. Holy Freakin' Shit Batman! This thing was more than thirty feet long and at least four feet wide! It was also wearing a gold earring!?! Stiff legged or not I jumped onto my chair and started screaming like a little girl!

She stepped to the edge of the porch and yelled, "Jean! Dis here's a nice young man come ta listen to an old woman's stories! If I tole ya once, I tole ya time an agin, if ya don't stop loosin ya temper round here ya ain't never gonna walk in my door like a man again, you ole fool, you!" For good measure, she poked him with her cane as he lumbered away.

She turned around and said to me "You can come down now, Chere. He's gone and he won't bother you no more no, if he knows what's good for him... Jes don' go swimmin." I swallowed my heart back down and carefully stepped onto the porch trying to remember how to breathe. She also sat back down and said "What was we talkin bout?" I said, "I think you were telling me about your girls?"

"Oh, thas my little Maddie and Adey, my great-grandbabies." She clearly loved them very much by the way her face lit up when she talked about them. "Where do they go to school?" She said, "Dey go to da school in Baton Rouge, but they might have to come stay wit me for a while. You gonna meet dem tonight, it'll be good fo ya." "Why?" I asked. She said, "Oh, lots a' people, they lahk to be 'round the gurls cuz dey are da Balance, yeah. An when ya have balance everyting jes works mo betta, yeah."

She was senile, I was sure of it. In an effort to steer the conversation back on track, I said, "Sooooo...about this research I am working on...are you related to Marie Hamilton?" She looked at me and said point blank, "Why do you wanna know?" I told her there was some question about an inheritance and that there was a chance that the wrong people were going to be getting something that might belong to her family if I couldn't prove that Marie had a child.

She thought about it for a minute and said clearly with no hint of the Cajun dialect, "I know my Marie just passed on, gone home to heaven...she was my little girl, headstrong and stubborn just like that old gator, she was." Then her accent returned and she continued "She done took off after de babe' was born."

Baby?! Yesss, grandbabies, Hell yesss!! Confirmation! Trying to hide my excitement, I asked "Did she in fact have a child then?" Stella again looked at me long and hard, "This story gonna help ya wit ya job, yeah?" I answered truthfully, "Yes, it will help me get the position as a serious journalist that I have always wanted, working for a major publication." Somehow I knew that I would get nothing if I lied to her now.

She sighed and said, "Ah guess it's better comin from somebody we can trus raht now. Dey's a'ready too many people askin too many questions and dey's gonna fine out where we are anyway. If Ah tell ya now, we can be ready when the others come." She looked down and started peeling her vegetables again and I gave her the time she needed to collect her thoughts.

9 WE'VE GOT A TAIL

Joe left MaMere's with a sinking feeling. He pushed the airboat as fast as it would go, damn near turned it over twice in his haste. When MaMere gave you a direct order like that, you didn't dawdle. Something bad was going to happen or she would have just arranged to have the school send them like she always did. That meant that she suspected that he would have trouble. The law was usually his gig and he did it well. If she asked him to call his Dad, the shit was definitely about to hit the fan.

His Dad had become a real hermit the last couple of decades and didn't interfere much in the going's on of his children's lives and concentrated on his research instead. His Mom however, was just the opposite, always sticking her little beak in their business. Not that he really minded, he loved her dearly, they were quite close.

As soon as he got to where he could get a signal he called his Parents. Lynne answered the phone and he told her what MaMere had said and how she acted. Before he could finish, Hawk had taken the phone. (He could hear a rat squeak from 1000 feet away) Joe didn't bother to repeat himself, but went on recounting what had happened. He told Hawk that he had been to the school several times before on errands for the girls so the current staff there shouldn't get suspicious if he went to pick them up without prior notice.

There was a long silence while Hawk thought about it and then he said that he thought it might be better if he got the girls instead. He would get the girls to come out to him and he would be able to get them without alerting anyone that there were even gone. He told Joe to muster the troops and then there was silence on the phone, he just hung up. Joe hated it when his father just flew away all the time without so much as a 'bye, thanks, or over and out. The old bird just didn't understand proper phone etiquette.

Joe got to his parents' house that evening to find that his Mom had already called his siblings, Jada and Jace. Jada had been visiting with her cousins Aundrea and Brianna at the time so they were there too. Joe also called Benoit's and got in touch with Lucky. He gave them a run-down of the situation. Lucky said he would get his Band mobilized and send word by way of the bayou to have everyone on standby until they gathered more intelligence. The next morning Joe also sent Aundrea, Brianna and Jace back out to MaMere's to act as security for the time being.

Lucky called back an hour or so later yowling in his excitement. His little group had discovered some rather unsavory characters snooping around where they shouldn't be in the middle of the night on his territory asking questions about the Eschte's and the Stranger that had come to town.

He also said his niece Cecile had notified him that several boats that looked like those vacation rentals were spotted all headed in the same direction, to Old Lady Lake.

Had they been moving slower, she said she might have shrugged it off as another one of those idiots who were trying to take over the swamp tours running several boats at a time without a clue where they were going or what they were getting into. But these caught her attention because they were moving real fast and almost all the boats were riding really low in the water like they were carrying a heavy load.

Lynne, Joe's Mother, heard what was happening and called her husband. Hawk told her to take all the children and other family members to some distant relatives in Austin, Texas. She started to argue that it would be too far away in case something happened.

Hawk thinking fast, quickly found a way to keep her safe. He knew that she would come to him no matter what he said unless he made her part of the plan. She was ferocious and fearless when her family was threatened.

He explained to her that if he needed reinforcements, she was to contact an old Indian friend of his that ran with a large notorious biker gang in that area. He would be able to round up the men he might need so he needed her there just in case with a backup plan.

Hawk also asked her to tell Joe that he had noticed that several of the groups of people they usually had trouble with were missing or moved out and that worried him because it appeared that someone was amassing a small army.

The next day, as Joe went about his preparations in town, he noticed that two men were following him and he again called his Dad and told him, "We've got a tail." Hawk told Joe to see how long they would hang with him and to act as if he were going about his regular rounds. Hawk also told him that he was now at the school, but there was something going on and security had been alerted when they had a break-in the night before and all the students records and been ransacked. The school was being overly cautious with visitors and double checking identification on anyone coming in or going out, including personnel working there.

Hawk finished talking with his son on the phone and let out a screech that the children would know was his call and waited for them to come to him. After a while the girls appeared at his side smiling in that mischievous little way they had. He bent down to talk to them on their level and asked them if they had heard from MaMere.

They said that yes she had told them that someone from the family would be coming to get them and bring them home. Petulantly they informed him that they had been waiting for him and wanted to know what had taken him so long. They asked him if he was getting slow because he was so old because they had been expecting him yesterday. With an understanding of their odd sense of humor he smiled and gave them a hug and asked if they remembered how to hold on for the flight to MaMere's. They giggled and jumped up and down. God, he forgot how happy these two little urchins always were. It made you feel good just to be around them. After this was over he would make it a point to spend more time with them. He had forgotten how much he actually loved children. He missed his own children now that they were grown and making their own way in the world. In order to get over his longing for grandchildren and the heartaches that come with difficult births, he had buried himself in research. Most people would be astonished to know that his current field of research was on infant mortality rates and genetics.

For now though, he still had these two little ones to play with. It wouldn't be long and they would be finally grown. He had noticed the changes since the last time he had seen them and they were subtle changes, but they were about to enter the next phase of their life cycle and he was afraid the innocence he had enjoyed seeing in them would disappear in the wake of knowledge and maturity.

Once Hawk had let him know they were airborne (with the girls manning the phone), Joe got everyone headed to MaMere's. Lucky and his band had joined him. Although they were normally a bunch of loners, they had developed their "Band of Big Cats" for lack of a better word for protection and guidance.

A large group of locals had also joined their effort to show appreciation for all that MaMere had done for them and their families over the years. Many of them owed her a great debt of gratitude for those services. Besides, no one wanted to be "inhospitable" to someone who could change their fortunes with the blink of an eye.

Heading down the bayou out of Dulac, they encountered a small war party just ahead. The big cats hadn't sunk their claws into anything in a while and were thirsty for blood so they volunteered to hang back and handle them while Joe and the others made their way to the island.

10 I'VE BEEN FISHNAPPED

Jamie was out with Sam and Max enjoying the afternoon sun and the beach. She had been experiencing a feeling of uneasiness all day. A little disoriented and foggy headed, she thought exercise, fresh air and getting her toes wet might help.

Jamie had been having a difficult time trying to continue her research and keep Sam and Max out of trouble at the same time. For some reason, Max seemed particularly interested in creating havoc with her friend Splash. Jamie suspected it might be a crush of sorts not unlike when humans entering puberty experience during those formative years. If you counted their growth rate, it would be about the right timing for those emotions to begin showing in their development. Sam didn't seem to have that problem yet. Maybe the females were different?

Every time Splash was out with her pod fishing, Max would start harassing them and dive into the water scaring the fish away. After one particularly bad incident, Splash came to her complaining. She said that the children were terrified of him and that he took pleasure in chasing and terrorizing them.

Jamie didn't tell her friend what she actually suspected to keep things on a civil level. Instead, she softened it a bit and told her that she thought that is was a sign of affection. After all, Max was strong enough if he wanted to hurt anyone he could have done so very easily.

Splash tossed her silvery hair and huffed indignantly that she could also do some damage to his testicles if he wasn't careful. Jamie promised that she would keep a closer eye on them.

Jamie noticed that although Sam wasn't pining after anyone like Max, she had gotten extremely cocky and was constantly showing her strength by trying to turn everything into a competition with her brother. It was just that reason that they were on the beach playing in the waves. Splash and her friends were harvesting their kelp beds today. If she could keep Sam and Max occupied, then maybe they wouldn't notice Splash's little group and things would settle down a bit until she could figure out how to keep Max under control. Just as she thought that, Sam began snorting and rolling around on the beach like a dog scratching her back in the grass on a summer afternoon. If she didn't know better, she might think that Sam had heard her thoughts and was laughing at her.

This was nice, she was just starting to relax and thought she might go for a swim. She had swum out about a hundred yards, when something grabbed her ankle and pulled her down under the water hard and fast. She had no time to breathe or even think. Just when she thought her lungs were going to burst, whatever had grabbed her broke through to the surface. Gasping and spluttering for breath, she turned and saw that it was Splash.

What the Hell do you think you're doing? You almost killed me! You haven't done that to me since I was a kid! Splash communicated to her that MaMere had been calling for her and for some reason, she wasn't able to get through. MaMere wanted her home pronto. Splash went to grab for her again and Jamie jerked away.

"Call for Asia and Phoros, they can take me across the ocean and allow me to breathe air. Better yet, let me get Sam and Max, they can get me there faster than any of you." At the mention of Sam and Max, Splash became even more agitated and told her that if she wanted them, then she was on her own.

Disgruntled and worried about the situation, Jamie gave it a second thought. She wasn't sure she could communicate to them where she wanted to go and how fast. They had a penchant for wandering off to play. The two of them might cause too much of a problem and if there was trouble, she didn't need more complications. On the other hand, if there was trouble, they might come in handy as well as Splash and her friends.

Jamie consented to calling the Orcas. After just a few minutes, they burst through the surface next to her. Splash had made her a harness and reins out of woven kelp and seaweed. She grabbed the reins and stepped onto their backs. If any human saw her right now, it would cause another media frenzy to see a woman riding two Killer Whales like a pair of skis. Then she would have to get Hawk to do damage control for her again and find some plausible way to say that it wasn't as it appeared. The Bermuda Triangle, Crop Circles, Sasquatch and Alien Abductions had been her best friend for a long time.

Jamie tried with all her might to call Sam and Max to ask them to follow at a distance in case of danger. She hoped that they would hear her. She was getting more and more concerned. She was always able to hear MaMere when she called or had a message for her.

A wave of warm air buffeted her hair and she looked up. They were indeed following. With Sam in the lead she tried to pour all her concern and worry into her thoughts and hoped that they would sense the seriousness of the situation and react in a way that would not complicate matters. Sam apparently got the message. She intercepted her brother on a diving run at Splash and then they veered off on a different but parallel course.

Relieved that at least she had back-up of her own, Jamie began worrying again about what was going on. After she got a little further out, she began to sense MaMere through her connection with Splash. MaMere comforted her some and told her that the girls were safe at the moment, but that she was needed at home because danger was eminent.

Jamie felt a surge and Splash yelled Hang On! She's giving us speed! They suddenly took off like a rocket. It's a good thing Jamie wasn't a weakling like most humans or she would have been shredded simply by the velocity at which they were going. Even the water seemed to be pushing them along. She felt like she was riding a tornado the way a cowboy broke a mustang.

It was all a blur to her for several hours and then the next thing she knew they were slowing down. They were in the Gulf of Mexico. She had traveled with Splash and her friends plenty of times before, but not at this pace. This was beyond anything she had previously experienced.

As they neared brackish waters, the Orcas slowed and she dismounted and let Splash and Bubbles guide her in. Yes, that's right I said Splash and Bubbles. They are, as you might have suspected water creatures or more precisely Nerieds.

Some might call them Mermaids, but when you use that term with them, it is a definite insult. Don't hint at the Disney Movie or you will get a severe dunking and will be informed that they are not related to Sea Cows.

Jamie named the women she knew as her Nannies when she was a small child because she couldn't put into a human voice the pronunciation for their real names. So, as a child might, she equated them with activities they enjoyed together.

Splash would swim up under her and throw her in the air to splash back into the water. Bubbles would dive deep and circle her in a ring of bubbles. Much like a Dolphin will do to create a bait ball, making Jamie squeal with delight as a very young child. Even now as an adult, saying their real names correctly was still beyond her capabilities.

11 THEY'RE GONE

Alan Crowley led his little empire like a well-oiled machine. His business was doing well...If you count the fact that he was draining cultist followers of their energy force and then feeding them to the Leeches. His "Leeches" in turn used those bodies to produce a growing army. With a small capital investment and a good marketing plan for recruiting purposes and a storage facility (that he obtained by intimidating the actual owners In to selling him for almost nothing) the returns on the finished product were quite sizeable.

When he approached Brady and divulged the extent of his operation and its' intent, Crowley asked him if he had any moral dilemma taking an active part in such an endeavor. Brady, quite aware that his refusal of their business arrangement would end with his death, told him that since his Son's exsanguination at the hands of the Eschte family, nothing other than his revenge in this world mattered to him.

Brady, also greedy for power and control wanted to be at the top of the proverbial ladder instead of the lowly position that his clan currently occupied in his race. He always felt slighted by the other clans because the only talent his clan possessed was to cause things to disappear, milk to sour, and dogs to go lame. Always malevolent, they were known to follow a family wherever they would flee. Crowley's plan to conquer all other races and use each particular talent to serve his own selfish agenda fit right in with Brady's need to become more than he was.

Crowley was rapidly gaining the reputation of running his little enterprise like a Mafioso Don and he was gaining ground in other areas of business as well. Torture, Blackmail and Human Trafficking were only a few of the lesser crimes he committed in order to secure the resources he required. He had an attitude of complete disdain for the human race and was convinced that the entire world should exist only to serve him and he would stop at nothing in order to achieve his goals.

Having sent for Brady to give him the results of their latest coupe de gras, he was furious to hear the results of their efforts. "Do you mean to tell me that you found those little brats the old woman has guarded with every means at her disposal for years and you let them slip through your fingers!" Crowley howled at Brady.

Brady fumed and responded, "Don't scream at me like I'm a stupid, mindless Troll to be led around by the nose! Let me remind you, that it was MY people who gave you the information that they even existed. I have risked my entire clan's existence in our race to help you find a way to defeat her! I told you when I agreed to take part in your plans that after her little tweety bird killed my Son, it has been my personal mission to see her and all of her kin dead. Do NOT think that you and your little teeny bopper cult scare me. My resources are more extensive than you imagine. I have given you the information you needed because you have the same goal in mind. Not because you think you can bully me or mine."

Brady, breathing hard with his tirade of indignation, paused to catch his breath and then continued as he struggled for his composure. "Now, this is what appears to have happened. Once we got the records from the school and believe me that wasn't easy, we found out that the place is guarded heavier than Fort Knox. Because it is guarded so heavily, it took a considerable amount of time to get one of our people in. We had to learn their schedules and find out when an extraction would even be possible.

When we got to the school to get them, they were gone. Before you ask, we couldn't determine what they were. We smelled Fae, Were and something else we couldn't identify. The little brats are resourceful too. Every time my agents would get closed enough to put their hands on them, they would somehow slip away or appear somewhere else entirely. In fact, the school didn't even realize they were gone yet. We probably only missed them by just a few minutes at most. They were in the Art room doing a project and told the teacher that they were going to the restroom. After a few minutes and they didn't return our team went out looking for them."

Crowley just sat in his big chair behind his desk with his arms crossed glaring at Brady. "Not only did you lose them, they were taken right out from under your nose." Crowley continued in an icy tone that made Brady wince in spite of his bravado. "Let's see if you have the intelligence to gather your people into a reasonable force of strength, Mr. I'm not afraid of the boogeyman that makes me wet the bed at night. The mindless Trolls you mentioned might be your saving grace at this point. Get them together now and get out of my office. I can't stand the sight of you right now."

Brady stormed out of Crowley's office slamming the door with a force that shook the walls. Crowley sat for a moment longer and picked up the ornate French phone on his desk and told the person on the line to have the Leech brought to him.

A few minutes later a very tall, very thin man walked in. He was dressed in a very expensive Armani suit. His long white hair braided in a que down his back. He entered the room with a silent grace of movement that would make a ballerina look clumsy. Power exuded from the man. Once seated, the man looked at Crowley with the red eyes of a predator, "You rang."

The man had always made Crowley nervous, but as long as he had leverage, he could control the monster. Crowley answered him, "The time has come to storm the island and take her by force. Do you have enough bodies to make that happen without Brady?"

Being a man of few words he simply said, "Possibly." When Crowley waited for more he continued, "Is Brady proving to be as worthless as we thought?" Crowley never liked being told his plans weren't perfect, answered, "No, he still may be of use. After all it has been his spies that have given me the most accurate and valuable information over the years. However, you may be right and their usefulness to me may be coming to an end. Have you ever tried turning one of them?"

The man didn't give him the answer he wanted but instead asked "Do you have the information I require yet?" Crowley didn't like being treated as an inferior and puffed himself up like the Peacock he was and said, "I told you I have the formula, but you will require the token of payment. Might I remind you that the particular item you require is rumored to be in the old woman's possession? Defeating her is also in your best interest as well as mine."

The man nodded and said, "So it seems. I would like more available recruits, but what I have will suffice. I might ask you if you have secured enough of your own resources to accomplish the task at hand, or do I have to lure more of the unfortunates to you?"

This time it was Crowley's turn not to answer directly. "Like you I am fairly certain I have what I require, though additional resources are always welcome." With a wave of his hand he dismissed the man with an "That will be all."

The man, obviously amused at Crowley's audacity, simply raised one eyebrow in response. With a small smile he raised himself from the chair and walked to the door. He opened the door to leave and turned and gave Crowley a humble bow and a wicked smirk, "As you wish… Master."

He turned and closed the door with such force that it shattered and fell to pieces, all the priceless artwork on the walls hit the floor and shattered as well. The man could be heard humming a little tune as he left the building.

After a moment or two, the phone on Crowley's desk rang. He hesitated before answering it, knowing who would be on the other line. "Yes Ma'am...No, I have not given him the information and everything is fine...Our plans have hit a little snag and we will have to go to the back-up plan, but I am confident we can accomplish the task. I am still in complete control of the situation... and the line was disconnected. He slammed the phone down on his desk, "God! I hate that woman!".

12 DID YOU SAY AN ANGEL, AS IN FROM HEAVEN?

After some time, Stella began telling her story. "My Marie was brought ta me by an Angel with blue and silver wings. She was a good and sweet little babe', yeah. She jes glowed a lil' too much and when she was a young girl, she caught de attention o' dat damned ole' Fairy boy, Aidyn Bauchan, an he was jes plain mean and rotten inside and out.

Dat whole family, dem, dey was jes as bad. Others lahk dem, dey good people, yeah, always helping families wit de normal daily duties dat dey need to make a house a home. But not deeze ones, dey is jes plain ole mean and cantankerous all de tahm."

"Anyways, one day Marie wanted to go to town and get a sto-bought dress fo da Fais Do Do. Dat's a dance party we have 'round here. So her brothers carried her ta town to git da dress. Dem boys, dey din want to be bothered by no girl stuff, no, so dey dropped her off at da dress sto and went ta do dey boy business."

"Dat Aidyn Bauchan, him, he was always spyin on my Marie. He watched dem boys leave and waited for Marie. When she comes out, he pushed her to da alley beside de sto and forced himself on her, my poor Marie. When he was done he tried to steal her lights too, but Hawk had heard her screams and come runnin to her rescue."

"Hawk, he sees dat damn Aidyn and in his madness he changes to his mighty bird form and claws Aidyn's eyes and face. Den he grabs Aidyn in his talons and flies straight up into de air a long ways and drops Aidyn, smashing his body into mud. People said de screams were awful and dey couldn't tell where dey were coming from until he hit de ground. By den, though, it was too late for Marie. She done lost her glow and she was planted wit his seed. She was never raht agin after dat day."

"When lil Jamie was born, Marie couldn't even look at de baby. She didn't want de child and took her away and lef here. We found de lil baby at de hospital, but we never heard from Marie again. Marie, she started dat school, yeah. She never forgot her MaMere and her special chirren."

Either I was completely losing my mind or she already had. "Excuse me for asking, but did you say Angel; as in, from Heaven?" She smiled and said "May, yeah." Stunned, I blinked until I could form words. "Uhh,huhhh... and Fairy, not as in a sexual preference insult, but as in the Tinkerbelle kind?" "Not Tinkerbell, no, das jes make believe but Fairy in the same sense of de word. And yes, thas what I tole you", she said continuing her chopping. "Oookaay....then the part about her brother, Hawk is it?" She chuckled, "Thas jes what we call him. His name is Robert, he is Joe's Daddy."

Wait a minute, I thought, what does that make Joe? Then I asked her "You said he changed into his bird form? You don't mean that he changed into an actual bird but that he used some kind of hang glider or something, right?" "Mais non, he changed into de ancient Thunder-Hawk, a bird, a very, very big bird. Dose birds, dey was wiped out before de white men came to dis land, but Hawk's parents were some of de last ones to breed and he carries de ancient blood of dat most Noble Family. So when he changes, he becomes de Great Thunder-Hawk.

Das 'bout ten times bigger, mebbe more, dan de eagles we have now. He can pick up a grown man with no trouble, but de gators, dey have hides dat are tick, yeah. Hawk, him, he's always messin with Jean Lafitte. Dey don't git along too well dem two. Hawk holds a grudge against Jean for a little spat dey had a long tahm ago."

There was no way in hell anyone was going to believe this story. I would never work again. My God! I have really turned into Karl Kolchak!

She touched my hand and leaned forward and said, "Now ya know why da story has to be tol' raht, yeah. Der is others that would want to know where lil' Jamie and da gurls are. Dey would hurt dem and use dem all up. We been keepin dis secret a long time and we trus dat ya will figure out a way ta tell da of story Marie so dat nobody gets hurt and dey won't be hunted by dose people greedy for dey gifts."

13 KOO-BEE-YAWH

The old woman was completely serious. Again, how to tell this story and have people believe it was suddenly getting harder and harder. I could see it now, my credibility ruined, they would label me as a nutcase and I would never be taken seriously as a professional journalist again. I would wind up writing for some small time local gossip column or worse yet, some alien hunting Hollywood gossip rag.

The only way that I could be able to validate my story would be to use the articles I had already found and try to get the birth certificate or affidavits of people present at the births. I would have to put a spin on the actual truth and not give complete identities or time frames without losing my integrity as an investigative journalist. I wondered if we could get a picture of Jamie aged to be a very old woman…. That might work.

Stella finished her chopping and stood up saying to me, "Now we gonna go to da kitchen. We gonna teach ya to make de soup jes raht." I followed her into the house. The furnishings were sparse, but neat and clean. The walls of the area to my right were lined in bookshelves with the exception of the wall for the fireplace. The shelves were packed with books. Some of them looked to be quite old and rare. Being a connoisseur of books myself, I stepped closer and saw that a lot of them were handwritten, rare or first editions and worth a fortune.

The fireplace encompassed most of the exterior wall. It had a large old-fashioned black pot or what looked like a witch's cauldron, but was probably just a large stewpot made for specifically for cooking in a fireplace and was hanging from a chain in the center. There were two large chairs on one side that looked to be antique and in good condition. There was a small intricately carved table between them covered with a glass framed oval top made from some kind of wood that looked like ebony and a type of red colored wood. The effect was striking in the richness of colors.

Opposite from the fireplace was a large rocking chair inlaid with what looked like hand-woven brocade panels. The entire place contained what I would assume was museum quality furnishings, but what do I know; I'm not an antique expert. There were several baskets next to the chair and another small round table at the height of the chair with a small vase of strange looking flowers in it. As I looked around I noticed that there were baskets of all shapes and sizes everywhere. The fireplace had baskets on the mantel and there were rows of drying herbs and flowers hanging above it.

To the right side of the large room stood a table that looked like it could have been THE Round Table from King Arthur's day. The carvings on the table also matched the chairs surrounding it.

The kitchen opened up from the left side overlooking the dining area. Every room but the bedrooms and baths were visible from the front door. Separating the house was a hallway that I assumed led to those rooms.

Entering the kitchen, I saw another smaller fireplace in the corner of the room with another pot hanging from the center. There were no modern appliances. Come to think of it, the place didn't even seem to have electricity. There was a large iron stove opposite from the corner fireplace with a pipe that ran up to the ceiling.

Something moved in a shadowy corner of the room on the floor. I looked a little closer and there was some kind of animal curled up on a small pillow with glowing green eyes. At first I thought that it was some kind of mutilated stuffed toy. I asked Stella what it was and she shrugged "Thas jest Scratchy Patchy, my cat." On closer inspection, the cat appeared to have one glowing cat eye and one regular green human eye. It must be the light playing tricks on me.

Looking up, I realized why the house seemed bright instead of gloomy. There were windows that opened up with a pull chain to admit light and ventilate the house. Like the other rooms, this room was lined in shelves from the counter up. These also contained books and most of them were really old as well. Bottles, jars, canisters and other cooking implements also occupied the shelves (I'm sure that the animal skulls and bottled bits were part of some type of collector's hobby).

While there were no modern accommodations, the kitchen appeared to function quite well. Even the sink had an old fashioned pump instead of a regular faucet. There was also waist high worktable in the center of the kitchen with shelves containing pots and pans on the shelves beneath it.

More drying herbs and plants hung from the ceiling of the kitchen giving the entire house an exotic, woodsy Caribbean smell. The effect was soothing and cozy. As she deposited our bowls on the counter, she pointed to the sink and said, "Wash your hands, son. Ah learnt from an old sawbones named Louis a long, long time ago dat washin de hands keeps de bugs outta de bodies, yeah."

While I washed my hands, she got out a large pot and put it on the stove. She bent over and opened a door beneath the top and blew on the coals inside. Immediately a flame appeared beneath the pot on top. She turned to me and said

"Come over here young man, Ah'm gonna show you how ta make de soup, an mebbe you'll learn some other things while we cook, yeah?"

"Firs, you get de animal fat lahk dis here and put it in de pan to heat." I asked, "What kind of animal is that from?" She laughed, "You can't be too picky, no. De fat is lahk de glue of life, yeah. It makes arryting slide together all nice like. Den, when ya git de fat hot enough, ya add de Trinity." I asked her what Trinity was. She said, "Chere, de Trinity is de place ya start... like the place ya was born. It takes de onions to make a body healthy, de cerry fa strenth, an de peppahs fa da spice in ya life."

"Like ya story, eh, you got to start wit de beginin. Now wit a good beginin, you can make any ole soup. De key is ta figure what kiiinda soup to make. You can make sompin' special lahk de Koo-be-yawh jes lahk we doin raht now. It has arryting in it to make people think 'bout what dey eatin, where dey are and where dey goin... or you can make Red Beans and Rice or Gumbo that is what de people 'spect from us Cajuns. It gives dem a full belly, is good to eat, but is plain to see what it is. Dey don' have to tink about where dey are or where dey goin. Dey is going home to rest dey full bellies. Dey don' ask questions either, dey jest know it was good and dey is satisfied with dat. Nuttin wrong wit bein satisfied, nuttin at all, non."

I looked long and hard at her and was not surprised this time to see the little lights twinkling in her eyes at me. "So what you're telling me is that you are going to give me the information I need to write a story that the public will believe without the "special" circumstances."

She pounded me on the back and said "Mais yeah, I knew I was raht bout you. You special too, ya jes needed to learn to see." I ran my hands through my hair and told her I didn't know how special I was, but that I appreciated what she was going to do for me. I still had enough of a scoop based on the existence of the living hiers.

She said, "Mais non... you is special too, lahk us. You can SEE." Again confused, I asked her what she meant. She said, "When you cut ya finger, what did ya SEE?" Blinking rapidly, I began telling her some of what I hallucinated... the edited version of course.

She nodded and said, "Dat be my Jamie, de girls momma. You been dreamin 'bout her fo a while now, yeah?" I nodded and she continued, "She knows der is danger to da gurls raht now an she's come ta help keep dem safe. Allons, come wit me, Hawk is comin in wit dem raht now."

14 IT WAS A GIANT BIRD!

Impossible, Joe left only an hour or so ago. He couldn't possibly have gone to town and driven to Baton Rouge to pick them up yet,... wait a minute, and how did SHE know? There was no phone here and I've been with her the whole time. I would know if someone called or came by to tell her. Now I know I stepped into a parallel dimension or something as soon as we left town.

Stella motioned for me to follow her back outside. We resumed our seats on the porch and she just sat there smiling and looking out to the sky above the swamp. I followed the direction she was looking in and noticed a small airplane headed in this direction. Ohhhh, Joe must have made some calls and had them flown here, yeah that was it. However, that was still a short amount of time even to have flown (unless you were able to go supersonic).

The plane started getting closer and I kept waiting to hear the noise of the engine and looked around for a landing strip, maybe it was the kind of plane that could land on water so I looked harder to see the pontoons instead of wheels and there weren't any. There was no engine noise and it was coming straight at us and fast something was hanging from the struts on the bottom and it looked like two people, children and then I realized what I was looking at. Holy Mother of Jesus! It WAS a giant bird! It was carrying the children in its claws! As it got to us, it circled once and let out an ear splitting shriek and swooped down and set the children on their feet. Then it flew up and landed on the roof of the house with a loud thump. Stella said, "Hawk has to get some pants on, come meet my babies."

MaMere! The girls shouted running toward her. They were about twelve or thirteen and at first glance, they looked like two girls that were very happy to see their Great Grandmother. They hugged Stella and danced around her telling her a million stories at once and crying about how much they had missed her and home. They told her they liked school but it was kinda boring being as old as they were but they found ways to keep busy.

The way they talked about the school, it sounded like they were two middle aged women instead of pubescent children, tired of the tediousness of a daily routine. However, in a much more spirited and inspired tone they told her they would rather stay here with her and go fishing all the time. What adventures they could all have together.

Stella stepped away from them and introduced them to me. She said tapping the girl with the snowy white, short and curly halo of hair. "Dis is our Madeline, she is our light. Madeline is the oldest daughter of Jamie, who was Marie's only child."

The girl was clearly outgoing and confident because she stepped forward and stuck out her hand. "Pleased to meet you, you can call me Maddey, and this is my sister Adeline or Adey for short. She is our night flower." How odd to refer to your sibling like that I thought.

While both girls were fair complected, Maddey had the bluest Eyes I have ever seen. Almost as if someone had taken pure pigment and painted them. Adey was the exact opposite of her sister, she was extremely shy and had blue black hair that was braided down her back almost to her feet. From the briefest glimpse she gave me of her eyes as she hid behind Stella, they were a vibrant green/gold like a cat.

While all this was interesting, I kept waiting for her to tell me about another person in the lineage. By my calculations, children of Jamie would be forty-three years old. Not the twelve and thirteen year old children I was currently being introduced to.

I asked MaMere, "Did you forget someone? Because these children are too young according to the records I have collected so far." MaMere's eyes twinkled again and she said, "Mais non, Chere. Dese are Jamie's gurls and Marie's grandchildren." Trying to wrap my mind around what she meant, Adey explained it all by saying in a wry tone that sounded much more mature than her looks portrayed; "We have aged rather well, don't you think?" Her voice now modulated with a smoothness that only maturity can give. With the introduction of giant alligators and living byplanes and now old women in little girls bodies, my world began to tilt and I began to laugh at the absurdity of my predicament.

Stella told the girls "This is Mr. Dan Rawlings, he is a reporter that is going to write about your Grandmother and your Momma." They both looked up at her with worried expressions. From behind us a deep voice resonated "Is that so."

Stella turned and started walking back to the house and said "An dis is my Hawk." Shit!! I got so caught up in the introductions I forgot it was in the house. He stood just a good bit taller than me and I am 6'1", with what I am proud to say is an extremely athletic physic. Dark Brown hair hung almost to his waist, a Roman nose, and dark skin. His eyes were piercing amber, the eyes of a predator. As he stared me down, I stood my ground. Not out of courage, but because I had heard that if you run from an animal it would attack. I hoped he couldn't tell the difference.

Stella stepped up to him and gave him a shove in the chest. "You an Jean, ya jes alahk you two, always scarin' mah guests." Hawk stepped between us and followed her inside the house. She said "Trus ya MaMere, son. It's tahm ta tie de loose ends dat cause us harm. Besides, Ah have a good feeling Mr. Rawlings here is jest de person we been needin."

Hawk said "Joe called and said that you wanted the girls here. What's coming?" She turned around and looked him in the eye, "De girls are in danger, we all are, Chere." Hawk ran a hand through his hair and sighed heavily. "This is all my fault, if I had only..."

Stella stopped him, "Shhhh, hush dat nonsense boy, dat damn fairy boy was gonna git to her one way or anothuh. Din' mattuh who was wit her, Marie was so headstrong... In the end though, she foun a man ta make her happy and das all dat matters."

She looked off in thought and said "We don't get to choose how de Lord was gonna bring us de girls. He made bringing dem into de world a difficult ting cuz we need to know how important de are to da world.

He put dem in our hands to protect and das what we gonna do."

"Did ya bring de game like I asked?" Hawk replied "Yes Ma'am, what are you cooking?" She handed him two knives and said "Koo be Yeah. Jamie will be here in a minute and I need to talk to her alone. Take Dan with you and get de game cleaned up. We done scared Mr. Rawlings here enough on his first day."

15 HAWK

Hawk turned to me and motioned for me to follow him. We went down the hall to another porch on the back of the house. It had a steel table with a sink complete with another hand pump. He turned and picked up a string with two ducks tied together that had been hanging on one of the posts and put them on the counter next to the sink.

He reached and got a couple of buckets and put them next to the sink. He handed me a knife and said "You ever clean game before?" I shook my head no and he sighed and said "I figured as much." "Here, I will clean the first one while you watch and then you can clean the last one. Everyone shares chores here."

I asked him about his accent and he looked at me for a moment and said "You saw me fly in and land on the house and you're concerned about my accent?"

What was I supposed to say, did you have a nice flight? He finally chuckled and said "No I wasn't born here, I was born around the New Mexico area I think, and my parents were of an ancient race assimilated into what is now known as Navajo."

I asked "But I thought you were Stella's Son?" He nodded and said "None of us are actually children she gave birth to. She found us and kept us safe, taught us many things, made sure we got a good education and accepted us no matter what we were. Hell, do I look like I have two Doctorates from Yale?"

Every time I turned around I was surprised by something here. Nothing was as it appeared. He began cleaning the duck. He put all the feathers in one bucket and the entrails in the other. He said "save the feathers MaMere likes to stuff pillows and blankets with them." I asked him what you do with the other bucket. He said

"that's Jean's." Confused again I said "Oh...
I thought you didn't like him." "I don't" he
said. "He tried to kill me when I first came
here."

"I was a young man when I came here
and he thought I had romantic feelings for
MaMere. I was very naïve about human
emotions and the intricacies of romance
between mates at the time. He couldn't
stand anyone getting close to her. He
came home one day and saw her kiss me
on the cheek, because I had given her a
deer for her ice box and he went ballistic.
Caught off guard and trying not to kill
anyone else I didn't defend myself and he
nearly strangled me to death.

I turned to him and said "I wanted to
ask someone, but I really don't know how
to put this into words, but is she some kind
of Witch or something? I am at a loss as
to what I have seen and been told since I
got here. I mean really, I have been told
about the actual existence of Fairies, and
Angels and right now I am talking to a man
who I have seen with my own eyes change
into or out of, to be exact, a giant bird.
And correct me if I am wrong, but when
you speak of Jean Lafitte, are you talking

about the pirate Jean Lafitte or maybe a grandson?

Hawk didn't even blink, he said "The pirate." I noticed he avoided answering the question about her being a witch. He continued as if I hadn't interrupted him. "Anyway, she pulled us apart and saved my life or more accurately his because I was on the verge of losing control and could have killed him quite easily but then she changed him into a gator and told him to get out of the house."

My eyes bugged out and I continued on my rant, "Oh great, to add to everything else I need to accept as reality, now we have an old woman that may or may not be a Witch and if you piss her off she will turn you into a toad! Hawk corrected, "Alligator."

"Wait, just how old are you?" I asked flabbergasted. He just laughed and said "I already told you, my mother and father were an ancient Navajo race, ancient meaning extremely old. I was born long before the white man settled this country. I first went to Yale as a student in 1823 and got my first Doctorate in what is now Behavioral Science. I went back and got my second Doctorate in Molecular Biology in 1950. I don't take my education lightly because of the state that MaMere found me. I couldn't read or write, I had forgotten how or maybe never had learned to speak anything other than my native tongue. I never want to be that helpless in my surroundings ever again so I went to school at MaMere's urgings. Even to this day I still manage to keep up with current scientific research."

"To answer your question about my age, all I can say is that I'm not really sure. My memory has large gaps after my parents were killed. I must have changed to my Hawk form and stayed that way a long time. I can remember back to more than three hundred years give or take a century or two."

Not sure what to say to that, I asked "How were your parents killed, if you don't mind my asking?" "Ahhh and now we meet the reporter" he laughed. He finished cleaning his duck and motioned for me to step into his place and to begin working on mine.

Strangely, cleaning and preparing dead animals wasn't as disgusting as I thought it would be. I guess knowing that this is food helps. At least I didn't have to kill it first.

That brought my attention to the fact that there were no bullet holes.

I asked about them and he pinned me with those piercing eyes and said "I can catch anything in the air but jet planes. I can even manage to get close to them on rare occasions. I am a very skilled hunter even with things on the ground, I don't need bullets." I felt the hairs on the back of my neck stand up.

He turned back to cleaning the ducks and continued, "My parents were killed a long time ago. As I said, my recollection of time and place is a little sketchy. All I can remember is that we lived in a cave in the side of a cliff. The ancient word for my people is actually Anasazi which is a Navajo word meaning ancient people who are not us. Anyway, an earthquake shook the mountain and my parents were inside. I watched them be crushed to death as the cave collapsed on top of them.

They had been teaching me to change in the air when it happened. I watched them die and that's the last thing I remember until soaring in the clouds one day, I saw a young girl being chased by some braves. I swooped down and caught her to bring her to safety, but she was so scared of me that I changed to comfort her... she never spoke again."

"How do you keep from being seen?" I asked finding my voice again. He said, "You ever look up toward the sun on a clear day?" It was my turn to laugh, "Never! It would blind me. I rarely even go outside on sunny days." Now he was curious and it made me feel a little more balanced to put him in the position I had been in all day.

"Ok, spill it. Tell me why you are special to MaMere" he said. I told him I didn't know what he was talking about. Then he said "Then tell me about yourself and I'll play reporter for a while." Fair enough he had told me some intensely personal things, the least I could do was tell him a little about myself as well. Besides, I felt comfortable around him for some reason, so it was easy to talk to him, something I rarely been able to do with anyone but my Mother and now that she has passed away.... Not so much with anyone else.

"Well, I'm from Sacramento, California. I went to school at Cal State, Got my degree in journalism at nineteen. I was home schooled because of a problem I have with my eyes and direct sunlight." He said "You don't seem to have a problem here and you don't look pasty like a vamp." Wait... are there really vampires too?!? At my nervous look he said "All in good time."

He motioned for me to continue and I began again, "There are tanning beds everywhere and I have some special goggles I wear to protect my eyes. The doctors think because my eyes are such a light blue that they may be reflecting additional light into my pupils. We have tried everything including colored and opaque contacts, nothing seems to work."

"You are right though, I don't seem to be having a problem with the light here. MaMere said she thinks it is because it is filtered through the trees so it is shady most of the time. I usually wear a hat to shade my eyes, but they haven't bothered me since I got off the boat." He just nodded and kept working on the ducks.

"Anyway, I completed my education very young and that presented a new set of problems as well. I had a hard time getting any kind of job other than errand or copy boy at such a young age. So, I started free-lancing for a couple of different papers and sending my stories in by mail. It was easier to submit my stories that way. Most of the time, they never knew they came from a 19 year old kid.

My stories were good and after a while, I got hooked on investigative journalism. I make a living, but barely. I enjoy what I do even though it is sometimes risky because I have to be on location when the stories develop. I have been to some interesting places both here and abroad. Everyone thinks that danger for journalists are in the war zones of foreign countries. Let me tell you we have war zones right here in the states too. I have learned to adapt and always be prepared for bright sun conditions.

Hawk nodded and told me that it really was impressive that I didn't run from him as most humans would. My desensitization to imminent danger from my job would explain why I didn't. I couldn't bring myself to correct his assumption.

My mom died about five years ago. My dad split before I was born. My mom divorced my stepsister's father when I was eight years old. She said he was too controlling, but I knew it was because he was an out of work Jock and brutes like that can't understand a little boy who won't go outside and throw the old pigskin around. To be fair, I guess he thought he was being a good stepfather and just thought I was a lazy little nerd.

It all blew up one day when he forced me to go outside and get some of what he called real exercise. He kept throwing a football at me until he hit me in the face and broke my nose. I couldn't open my eyes to see, let alone to catch a football or defend myself, I was blinded.

My Mom came home from work and found us in the back yard. He was standing over me yelling for me to get up calling me a "Momma's Boy". To make a long story short, she kicked him out and my retinas were damned near fried. So, from then on, it was just the three of us. My sister Sandra went to her weekend visitations with him but when he re-married, that stopped too. He always was a jerk and always will be I guess."

"You seem fit" Hawk said. "Well I actually like sports. I'm a good swimmer as long as I can go to an indoor pool. I wrestled, played handball, and took enough classes in martial arts that I have belts in Karate, Hapkido and Jujitsu. I like learning the different styles of self-defense they are so much an art form... and it has helped to get me out of some sticky situations in the past."

Smiling he said "So that explains a lot. You have strength and agility. It shows in the way you walk and stand. When you first saw me and realized what I was you jumped about three feet in the air. It also means that you aren't fat and lazy like most that are confined to a life indoors. You chose to exercise your mind and your body instead. However, I could hear your heart beating like a jackhammer when I landed. I guess you just haven't experienced nature much."

Experienced Nature!! Who the hell did he think he was!? Oh!, right! He was a giant Hawk that could cut me in pieces in the blink of any eye. Of course I was scared! These people act like all this is perfectly normal and that I'm the one that should be studied.

That's it, they are all insane and I have somehow slipped into another dimension.. Do,do,do doo and this is Rod Serling and you have just entered.. the Twilight Zone. How was I going to get any of this on paper was a mystery to me.

I guess he could see that I was getting frustrated, but he kept waiting for me to respond. I said "Duhhh, where I come from men don't fly and certainly not in the form of a ferocious giant bird that could kill you in the blink of an eye!

He laughed and said "Yeah well maybe you've got a point. I'm not used to having to avoid being seen when I come here. You startled me too."

He leaned against the sink and watched me try to chop off the head of the duck as he had done. I asked him "Does it hurt to change like that?" He said "No, it's kind of like putting on a jacket when you are cold, it's instinctive to change. I feel better, after a change and I can heal faster if I am wounded if I change."

"Are there any more like you?" I asked. "I'm not sure, maybe, but I haven't seen any in three hundred years. I keep looking though", he said.

"From what I have learned from the legends, we are monogamous and immortal as a race. Unless we are mortally wounded, we cannot die of natural causes. Therefore, it stands to reason that mating is always for love. Birth rates are very low so finding a mate with the strength and longevity to procreate is rare."

I asked if he could mate with others that were not Birds. He said, "I assure you that in this form, I am a fully functioning human with all the anatomy required to do the job. I said that we are monogamous not incapable.

I have found another with a long life span, perhaps not as long as mine, but I have lived a long time already. By the way you did meet my son Joe right?"

Oh! Yes! I had forgotten so much had happened. "So, is Joe... like you?" He sighed heavily and said "No he took after his mother, Lynne. We are what you might call Shape-Shifters. Lynne is a fox and a falcon. She is a rare in that she has two spirit totems, thus making it possible for her to be my mate. Without confusing you more than you already are let's just say that her uniqueness made it possible for her to become my mate even though she is not another Thunder-Hawk."

We have the ability to transform our human selves into our spiritual being or totem animal if you follow Indian Lore.

We are human in every sense, but the Indians theorize that all humans have a spiritual self. Humans that can't change are just not strong enough in spirit to tap into it and shift to another form. Some people carry the characteristics of their spirits in everything they do. You might have heard some describe someone that was "as mean as a snake", "as mad as a bull" or "as sly as a fox". It is these abilities that have always been a part of us for centuries, but as our human minds grew, we relied less and less on our spiritual abilities so that now only the euphemisms remain. Many religious beliefs hint at it and folklore remembers, but for most the spirit is now too weak to acknowledge the ability."

Interesting concept, but I still think I am in the Twilight Zone. "How do you know all of this?" I asked. He said "Let's just say that I have had plenty of time to do a little research into the matter."

I asked him, "If all this is true, then why isn't the world chock-full of Were People? (or is it? I thought to myself). He said, "Birth and Conception is a complicated process for most Weres. It is rare that the child survives either part of the process much less the trials of the first few years until puberty. You might want to remember though, animals usually have litters, not one birth at a time so that helps." My curiosity overran my mouth and I blurted out, "Do you give birth to human babies or animal babies or do you lay eggs?" Upon seeing my immediate embarrassment at my rudeness, He was gracious enough to overlook it and continued, "Let's just say we have been lucky to have Stella's and Jamie's help with our children and the birthing process."

"While your theories are interesting, that brings me to another question. I heard Stella talk about God and Angels. How do you explain that?"

He nodded and replied "Good question. I wondered about it myself many times. I have come to this conclusion; Christians have learned about God from the Bible. A book written by men and edited over time by politics and organized religion. While it is correct in the teachings and lessons that it was meant to convey, there are some interesting facts that have been omitted... let's say due to graphic content."

"We have learned throughout history that modern man shuns or fears that which he does not understand. The Salem Witch Trials are a prime example. These poor women who had discovered how to perform simple healing techniques gleaned from their Grandmother's recipes, research and experimentation with items found in nature and provided by God himself were tortured by men who were Jealous of their skill or of being usurped in their positions and revealed to be the Charlatans that they actually were."

That gave me a lot to think about. Something else I had been wondering was, if he was more than three hundred years old, then how old would Stella really be? I realized that no one had actually given me an age, just that she was more than 100. How much more was the question. I have got to sit down and do the math on all of this.

Hawk gathered our ducks and said, "by the way, Hawk is just a nickname." He stuck out his other hand and said "I never properly introduced myself. Robert Brown-Wing Eschte, pleased to meet you." I shook his hand and we carried the game inside to Stella.

16 SHE PINCHED ME ON THE ASS!

Standing at the stove with Stella was the woman of my dreams... er, uh... vision. She was tall, nothing really special about her build except that she looked athletic.... Oh, who am I kidding... she was a knockout.

She was tanned and had legs that went on forever. Her hair was a medium brown shoulder length and a little on the wild side. She had a couple of silver rings in her hair to tame it away from her face. She had dark eyes that sparkled with mischief. She had the most expressive face I had ever seen.

The first thing she said to me was "So, how many times did you shit your pants today, Dan my man?" Stella elbowed her in the ribs and said "Jamie Lee! Behave yourself, Chere! Mr. Rawlings here is our guest!"

Then she added slyly from the corner of her mouth "Ah almost thought we was gonna have a mess ta clean up when he met Jean Laffite, aaiieee! Chere, tee babe!" Then Jamie and Stella both erupted into hilarious laughter.

Jamie sauntered over to me and did a slow assessing circle around me and said nice butt and then she pinched ME on the ass! Never having been one of those Neanderthal men who did that sort of thing to women, I was a little embarrassed to be on the receiving end. I turned around and was about to protest when I saw Jamie barely holding her laughter in check with that wicked little smile and said "You hide an athletic body under those baggy, nerd clothes... Well, maybe you won't be such a pansy-ass after all. Only time will tell. A good body is useless if you don't know how to use it."

Flustered, I was having trouble getting my emotions under control. This was the woman that I have fantasized about for so long and now here she is, in the flesh and pinching my ass and judging me. Having been picked on by neighborhood kids who also mistook me for a weakling, I trained my mind and my body to avoid getting my ass kicked every day. As I got older, I learned to be good natured and have a quick come back to most insults or taunts deflecting violence in most cases. But right now, I couldn't think of anything to say let alone make my mouth form anything that could be comprehended.

Seeing her like this had hit me like a Mac Truck. I haven't been this tongue tied since I was in the fifth grade and Melissa Lewis and I were paired in the school play. She announced that she was going to find the girls and turned to leave and then stepped back and leaned in and whispered in my ear, "Yep, just as firm as you appeared in MY dreams too." Then she sauntered out the back door.

I thought I was going to swallow my head. She had the same dreams!! We had done things in those dreams. Blushing furiously at having been called out by a woman I just met on the most erotic things I had ever experienced or imagined in my whole life... even if they were just dreams was just too much for a guy to deal with and keep his cool.

Hawk slapped me on the back and shook his head, "That girl will say the first thing that comes into her brain, don't take offense. No one has ever been able to make her understand the meaning of the word Tact."

Stella spoke up and said "Now Hawk, you better than anyone knows dat she does dat to keep people from seein how sweet and vulnerable she is." Hawk huffed and said, "Yeah, well she bites too."

Then he turned to me and said, "Do you know when she was only five years old, we hired a tutor to begin her lessons. After only two days she had bitten a chunk out of the poor woman's leg so deep it required a skin graft from the woman's buttocks to repair it. No, that girl is headstrong and always will be. I'll never know how the Nereids were able to control her on that island long enough for her to become a Physician."

"She's a doctor too?" I asked incredulously. Stella said "Mais yeah, Chere, she done got to de island and saw all dose chirren eat up wit disease and couldn't stand it, non. She studied hard at de hospital and den went to de school in New Zealand to learn more so she could help dem babies."

I looked back to Hawk for a clearer explanation and he said, "There is a remote island in the vicinity of New Zealand that is inhabited by a native population where Jamie moved to after the girls were sent off to the school.

When she arrived there she soon discovered that the infant mortality rate was well over fifty percent. She was determined to discover the cause and after considerable research, has found that it is neither caused by diet or the environment, but by a chromosomal abnormality that she hopes she can correct by means that are not available in normal human research facilities."

MaMere nodded her agreement and turned back to Hawk and said "By de way, Chere, I want you to know you might have company in de sky soon." Hawk looked at her sharply and said "What do you mean by company?" She smiled and said "You jes remember your manners. It's been a long time since ya had to share de skies wit anyting big as you in it... living dat is."

Hawk looked at Stella a long minute

and began cursing and stripping as he went running out of the house shouting over his shoulder, "If she brought anything to this island that is dangerous, I will kill her myself! That girl is going to be the death of me!" and he jumped off the front porch naked one second and feathered and airborne the next.

Jamie stepped outside and called to her girls. After a minute she felt them stalking her, a subtle movement in the grasses, a small scuff of cloth against a tree and Jamie braced for the attack, a moment of pain at the memory that these stalking games were a necessary part of their survival.

Caught off guard by her lack of focus, Jamie was hit in the back by a flying mass of black hair that had launched itself from the trees above her. She almost recovered when the little snowy haired chameleon struck and hit her in the legs for the take down.

The three went rolling to the ground laughing and tickling and wrestling. They played for a while and then Jamie sat up and gathered them close in her arms and said, "Maddey, Adey, I have a surprise for you, but you must keep it a secret even from MaMere. Do you girls understand?"

The girls nodded, but Maddey said " We keep telling you we're not babies Mama we're almost grown and we don't have to tell her, she already knows." Jamie smiled a little and said to them "Well you will always be my babies even when you're old and gray. Maybe we can try to keep it a secret anyway."

"Speaking of Old, I have brought something that hasn't existed since when MaMere was a young girl like you two are now." Adey looked at her Mother and said, "Why do we have to keep it a secret from MaMere?" Jamie answered "Because MaMere might be mad at me again for not leaving the old things alone. She gets pretty mad when I meddle with things from the past. But I think this will be ok, because they will protect us and we might just need them right now."

Maddey said "We know that there is trouble coming, Momma. We have had dreams but Adey and I know what we are gonna do when it comes so you don't have to worry about us at all." Jamie looked at Maddey and said and "just what are you going to do?" The girls both giggled and said in unison "It's a secret!"

Jamie reached down and shouted in her Mommy Monster voice "Then I will perform tickle torture to get you to divulge your secrets!" and they fell to the ground wrestling, tickling and laughing once more.

17 DRAGONS!

After tickle time was over, Jamie stood up and said "Ok, time for your surprise. We will have to go to the swamp side to get them." They walked down a trail that was beginning to become shrouded in fog now that the sun had set. When they came to the edge of the swamp, Jamie made a gurgling noise in her throat and waited. The girls stood silently beside her waiting.

Then slowly they saw movement on the water coming toward them. Adey said "Momma, if you got us some gators Jean Laffite is gonna be mad and he won't give us rides on his back anymore." Jamie frowned and said "You don't need to be playing with Jean, he can be easily provoked and might hurt you even if he doesn't mean to."

Maddey shook her curly head vehemently, "He's our friend and he's lonely, he doesn't have anyone to play with. He takes us to his secret places and we have the best fun together having our tea time."

Alarmed, Jamie knelt down to talk to the girls seriously "What kind of secret places?" Adey laughed and told her in a child's very serious tone, "Why where his buried treasure is of course. We can't tell you because we took the Pirate's Oath. He lets us play with all the jewels and necklaces. There is even a crown and we can be princesses. Our Tea Set is gold and was the Queen of Spain's a long time ago."

Jamie stood and looked at the joy that shone in their eyes at the description of discovering the old pirate's treasure. Then she thought to herself, Hell she might even enjoy playing dress up with real treasure herself. She thought about it for a moment longer wondering if she had misjudged the old pirate and changed back to the original subject, "Well, he might get mad anyway because these are not gators."

Then what had looked like two large alligator snouts coming toward them started rising up out of the water. They rose up and up and up. "Dragons!!!!" the girls both squealed together. Jamie started to reach out and stop the girls from running forward so as not to startle the Dragons, but she was just a split second too late.

The girls rushed forward and as soon as they reached the Dragons, they leapt up onto their heads as natural as mounting a horse. They hugged the dragons and immediately imitated the gurgling cooing noise that Jamie had first made and hugged the great beasts. Jamie shook her head and crossed her arms to watch them and said, "I should have known."

"How did you find them, Can they fly? What are their names? Can we bring them to the school? Can we scare the kids with them? Oh, pleeease! It will be so much fun to see those kids run!" both girls intoned. Jamie answered "Hang on, one question at a time. No, you can't take them to school. You have tormented those children too much already. You must remember that just because you are bored with the humans and even though you are much older and smarter, you must still treat them with respect. You will learn how to blend in and be safe by being with them."

At their looks of contrition, Jamie wasn't fooled but continued, "I found their eggs buried at the bottom of the ocean in the ruins of Atlantis. I was swimming there with the Nereids looking for some of the medical scrolls that might have survived. I was on the verge of a breakthrough with the disease that is killing the babies on the island."

"I took the eggs back to the island and put them in an incubator to see what would happen. At first nothing at all happened then I noticed that the corrosion on the shells was flaking off more and more with the added heat. The shells remained completely intact and looked healthier the hotter I raised the temperature in the incubation chamber. So I took a chance and decided to risk it all and put them in a kiln on 1500 degrees for 8 weeks.

Each week that passed the eggs continued to look healthier, but after two more weeks and no change, I was about to give up, I took them out to observe them one last time and sat them on the table. While I watched them cooling I began to hear an odd scratching noise in the shells. I watched a little while longer and the shells began to crack open.

When they stuck their heads out, they began eating their own shells. Then they started racing all over my lab looking for food. What a mess! Anyway I believe they think that I am their Momma too the way they always follow me around. I really didn't have much choice to bring them with me they would have tracked me down eventually."

Jamie laughed at another memory and told them, "When they were first hatched they were more trouble than you two. They destroyed my lab several more times until we learned to communicate with something like a combination of body language and sign language."

"They grew at an incredible rate and I had to take them hunting in the ocean several times a day to satisfy their growing appetites. The Nereids practically abandoned me right after they hatched saying that they didn't want to be mistaken for Dragon kibble. They get along fine now, mostly, but the Nereids still won't come anywhere near them when I'm not around."

"I have named them Samantha (Sam for short) and her brother Max because on the first day they were born, I was watching cartoons and Sam perked up whenever Yosemite Sam started calling his dragon and Then later when the Movie Mad Max came on, it reminded me of how the male would watch his sister and ambush her, so I named him Max."

"They have already protected me from a couple of close calls on the island from the local Fae getting nosy about their presence. They actually thought that Sam and Max could be claimed as Fae property. It was kind of amusing to them, I assure you."

"Apparently they are immune to magic, even Fae magick and fire. Their scales are extremely hard. It is impossible to pierce their hides. They are heavy but, they can fly and they like to sleep in a cave or in the ocean. They have gills like a fish so they can breathe underwater like the Nereids."

"I brought them to you because they seem to be able to communicate with each other just like you two do, telepathically.

Can you reach them with your minds?" Maddey and Adey looked at each other, puzzled and then back at Jamie. Maddey said, "Yes, we heard them answer you when you called for them. Couldn't you hear them too?" Jamie said, "My powers are a little different, I can feel them and understand them by the vibrations of their emotions but not by actually speaking with them. It's nice to know that they have been communicating with me all along."

"You will have to watch out for Hawk, I don't know how he will react with another predator as big as he is in the skies. Remember that Hawk is your Uncle and loves you very much so you must control the Dragons so that they don't harm him." Adey looked at Jamie with a pleading look and said, "Momma, if we train them really well, they can protect all of us and then we won't have to go to school in Baton Rouge and we can come live with you. We won't ever have to be apart again."

Jamie sighed and said, "We've tried that before and the LeFey's got suspicious and that's why we had to separate in the first place. I don't like being apart from you two either, but we are a bigger target altogether. I had hoped that they would be the solution to our problem, but it is too early to tell. That's why we have to keep them a secret. The fewer people that see them, the better protected we will be."

.

18 THEY'RE MY KIDS DAMNIT!

"Your secret is out." Jamie and the girls jumped at the sound of Hawk's voice as he touched the ground. "I've kept you safe all these years, but Lord knows I could use some help." Hawk sighed watching the dragons. "When did you spot them?" Jamie asked. "While you three were playing in the back of the house." Hawk replied. Jamie mused, "It figures they couldn't be trusted to lay low even for a little while."

"We've already met. They are surprisingly intelligent. Apparently, Dragons have a collective memory synapsis. They are the true historians of this world. Their memories and knowledge are stored in their DNA. They are not skilled yet, but they do have the knowledge of being warrior protectors…As with everything, practice makes perfect."

Hawk continued, "I have agreed to help them train, but our time is short and there is great trouble brewing. Apparently, you are not in trouble with MaMere, because they telepathically called to you to find them. Kind of like a homing beacon."

"Sorry to rain on your parade but MaMere also helped them find you, you didn't actually find them. However, they are impressed with the way that you anticipated their needs to hatch and solved the problem of intense heat to activate their life systems. They have a misguided notion that you are their human."

"Can we help train them too?" chimed the girls. Hawk smiled at them and said, "Yes, you need to learn to ride them in the air. But first I am going to have Justin, make harnesses for you so you don't fall off. You can help me get their measurements in the morning." Squealing with delight, the girls ran down the path back to the house to tell MaMere the news.

Hawk turned to Jamie, "Tonight, we will set up our defenses with their help. They have also alerted Jean Lafitte and he will be working with us. Jean, nasty, self-centered old pirate that he is, has always been a fantastic strategist. He and I have uh... formed a truce for the time being."

Jamie looked surprised, "You spoke with Jean?" Hawk said "No, but he spoke to me through them. Someone here is a strong empath and is giving me the mental strength to link to Jean through them." Hawk said "You might try to actually communicate on a mental verbal level now with the Dragons while this is possible and develop a better understanding of them." Jamie closed her eyes and concentrated for a minute, and her eyes flew open and she said "You're right! We CAN actually communicate now."

Realizing the importance of the information he had just given her she was silent for a minute longer thinking about the implications of the situation and asked him "You're the great and mystical Indian Shaman and you mean you can't tell where the link is coming from and you're sure it's not me?" He shook his head, "No the link is stronger than yours but completely wild and it is someone or something here but I don't think they are aware that Jean and I are tapping in on them."

"Does Jean still hate you?" Jamie asked. Hawk said, "Yes. However, my marriage to Lynne did dispel his jealousy of MaMere. He still blames me for being the reason for having to live as a gator." Jamie stared at Hawk for a long moment and said, "Well maybe you two can work things out later. Surely it can't be the reporter, he's human. There must someone else on the island that we don't know about."

"However, Jean would have felt the vibrations of someone new on the island. If it were my abilities, you would have been able to talk to him all along, so that leaves that explanation out."

He asked her "By the way, why haven't you tried to talk to Jean before?" Jamie hung her head and said, "To be honest, he always kind of scared me as a kid because he was always angry and watched MaMere so closely." He huffed and said "You, scared of anything, now that's funny." Hawk said "Maybe, but I don't think so. I have my suspicions about who it might be, but it is so far-fetched that I don't want to say right now."

"Time is of the essence and I need to take these two into the air. You go catch up to the girls and go back to the house. I want to make sure no one is watching you and no more sneaking off into the swamp without telling anyone for the time being."

Jamie's face reddened, "I am not a child and I am perfectly capable of protecting my girls... without you. You are not my father and you can't treat me like a little girl anymore. When are you ever going to see that?"

Hawk sighed, "Look this is not like the other times ok, even MaMere is worried. Please don't be difficult. I love you like you were my own child and I don't want to see anything bad happen to you. You have a penchant for finding trouble by being so impetuous and headstrong. This is serious, if not for me; please remember we are all trying to keep Maddey and Adey safe."

With tears about to brim over, Jamie turned on him and shouted. "You think I don't know that! These two girls are the only thing that has kept me sane all this time after Barry was killed. Don't you think I want to be able to be with them all the time and not have to sneak visits with them? Do you know how hard it is to see them leave every time? Do you really know what I went through when those Boggarts and Storm Spirits attacked and forced me off the road and kidnapped me." Tears streaming down her face she tried to wipe them away and laughed sarcastically, "All because I was part Fae and subject to their rule. They actually tried to sentence me to pay for my own Father's death with my servitude."

"As soon as the Nereids got me out of those chains, I clawed my way back, but my children were gone and I had no idea how to get them back." She stepped closer to Hawk and lowered her voice and looked him in the eye. "Do you know how that even feels? What was I going to do, send out a Missing Children report and alert the entire world to what caused that the sudden shift in the balance of the world magic? No, I couldn't even do that could I? I just had to hope that they were in good hands and not having their little lives being siphoned off for their power."

When I saw that man getting the girls out of the car, I felt like someone was ripping my heart right out of my chest. I am just thankful that the man that rescued them was human and had no clue as to what kind of power they possessed, but he helped get my girls to safety and for that I will always be grateful to that man.

"Trust me, I know that protecting them every way I can is necessary because being part Fae, they can smell my blood and track me and if I am with them, they would be after them faster than I could blink." A little calmer now, she had stepped back and looked out in the distance. "I want to be able to take them with me to my own island so we can be together all the time. I want to be a true mother and not like a visiting aunt. It is hard on me. It is hard on them too you know."

"We can speak telepathically, yes, but it's not the same thing as being able to hold them and put them to bed at night. They are MY kids Damnit! and I want them with me. I will do anything to get them and keep them permanently and whether it meets with your high and mighty approval or not, these dragons may be the solution to being with my kids!" and Jamie stalked off down the path back to the house.

19 PERHAPS WE CAN SAVE HIM FOR AN AFTER-DINNER SNACK?

Hawk turned back to face the Dragons and said to them, "I just want to keep them all safe. I have always tried to protect her just as hard as she protects her own children. I will continue doing so...even if I have to protect her from herself. Do I hear any objections?" The dragons gave him their consent with their silence and remained very still.

Hawk let out a long breath of air and said "Then, shall we be off?" and he jumped up into the air like a rocket and the dragons were right behind him trailing half the swamp water in their wake.

After going through several air maneuvers and aerobatics, they practiced flying in formation synchronizing their movements with the precision of an experienced squadron. Hawk called in his son and daughter, Justin and Jada for practice as well. Justin was also a hawk, but a regular hawk and Jada was an Owl.

He put Justin and Jada on point with Sam and Max following in a triangle formation behind them. Together they ran drills of spotting targets on land and in the air and running mock assaults. Justin and Jada would spot the targets and circle them to herd them together and then Hawk would make and slashing dive and flush the prey out of the water or wherever their hiding place was and the dragons would swoop in and roast the remains with their fiery breaths. This strategy would be very effective in combating large groups of invaders on the ground.

Then he put them all to work practicing claw to claw aerial combat. The Red Baron wouldn't have survived ten seconds with this group. Even the smallest, Jada was lethal. She went straight for the eyes and jugular. Because she was so small she was often underestimated for her tenacity.

One weak point for the dragons was their stamina for flying while firing. They used up a lot of energy when they breathed fire and would subsequently tire more easily because of their bulk. It was right as Hawk had discovered this inadequacy that they spotted the Fairies headed toward MaMere's island. They were riding large alligator snapping turtles. Almost invisible in the water at night, it was actually Jean who got their attention.

It appeared that the fairies were a scouting party and Jean had headed them off, creating enough of a disturbance on the water to catch Hawk's attention.

Hawk called to Jean and told him not to kill them, but to capture them to find out what they wanted and how much they knew.

While Hawk had been giving instructions to Jean, Max swooped down and simply dove in a kamikaze maneuver and ate the fairy and the turtle in one large gulp. He swooped back up into the air and blew a little blast of fire followed by a smoke ring to show that he had replenished his energy to generate enough fuel to stoke his fires once again.

Sam started moving toward the remaining fairy in the same diving maneuver as well when Hawk headed her off and told her that he needed that one unharmed. Snorting with frustration, she continued her descent into the water and came up behind the turtle-driving fairy and gave them a little heated incentive to follow Jean's lead back to the house.

The Fairy, as Stella explained to me or more appropriately Boggart as there are many types of Fae, was indeed a member of the family of Boggarts that had attacked Marie and had always tormented Jamie as a child.

Because of Jamie's mixed Angel and Fae blood, they were always able to scent her or feel her presence when she was near. The leader of their clan Brady Bauchan was Aidyn's father.

He had arranged to have Jamie kidnapped when the girls were still babies to avenge his son's death. Fortunately, he didn't have a clue what Marie really was nor Jamie and certainly not the girls. If he had all would have been lost a long time ago. Nereids saved Jamie and fought the Boggarts, but they were too late to recover the girls.

So, for a time Stella had arranged for them to live with humans as a disguise. It was hard on everyone, but it worked. With that in mind, the Boggarts were usually a little more cautious about approaching MaMere's house. This attempt was a little bold even for them.

When they got to land, Sam and Max filed in behind them as rear guard. Then just as Hawk was about to start interrogating the Boggart, Sam and Max started to bubble. They started transforming.

Sam made growling noises and bones started crunching and grinding. Max, grunting extended a claw that turned into fingers and then they started shedding their skin and scales.

As the skin hit the ground it began to disintegrate to a fine sparkling dust. This continued until they stood up as a young girl and a boy.

Sam was very thin and wiry with long brown hair. Her eyes, however, remained the green eyes and slitted pupils of Dragon's eyes and she still had dragon teeth and claws for hands and feet.

Max, finishing his change into a young man had blue eyes, blonde hair and normal pupils with human teeth. He coughed and said "She needs to eat live flesh and so she can fully change, dude." "Why haven't you changed to your human forms before now?" Hawk asked. Max said, "There was no need to before." Perplexed, Hawk asked, "Is there anything else you can do?" Max answered, "I don't know, what do you want us to do?"

Sam grunted in frustration and Hawk said "Will the turtle work for food? (An alligator snapping turtle is an ancient turtle that looks prehistoric with its ridges and spikes on its shell and sharp beak of a mouth.)

Sam nodded and Max said, "Sure, her teeth are still sharp enough to pierce that shell, but it might be a little messier not being able to swallow it whole. The Boggart would've been easier, man."

Hawk chuckled and put his arm around Max's shoulder in a gesture of camaraderie and said, "Not just yet, I need to talk to him first. Perhaps we can save him for an after-dinner snack."

Then quick as a wink Sam snatched the turtle by a hind leg and ripped the shell off like opening a bag of potato chips. That turtle was as big around as a child's swimming pool. She looked up for just a second and turned around and stepped back to the water and started shoving meat and other turtle parts into her mouth.

They waited in silence for her to finish and the Boggart started shaking as he watched her eat. She had washed all the blood off her body and walked back to them with normal hands and feet and dark brown human eyes.

Hawk said to them, "At some point tonight we need to have a long talk about your abilities." "That's cool" Sam said, "We will tell you whatever you need to know." Hmmmm... that was just a little too cryptic of an answer for Hawk's liking and he stored that little tidbit for future reference. He was going to have to watch them closely. Something was definitely not as is appeared with them.

The Boggart now trembling furiously and giving off a stench of rotten fish with his fear induced sweat kept a good distance between himself and the Dragons. Jamie walked up with a pair of pants for Max and a man's shirt for Sam to cover their nudity. Apparently nudity is not a big deal around these people. I was the only one blushing.

When they were dressed, she gave them a hug and said let's go inside, everyone is waiting for us. They all turned and followed Jamie across the yard to the house, including Jean Lafitte bringing up the rear.

MaMere and I were still standing on the porch watching. As Jamie reached Dan she smiled and said, "Don't worry about it, I might have swooned as well, if I were human. Fortunately, I'm not, but when they came out of the water and started changing, I was quite surprised too. I'm sure you have had more than your share of surprises today." I smirked and said, "After my head stops spinning, can you find something around here to prove to me that I am not in a parallel dimension or that I am not having some type of psychotic breakdown."

Jamie slapped me on the ass and said "Oh will you get over yourself already. You're fine and you are still on the same planet you were born on, this is all just a bit much in the beginning for anyone. I was just teasing you a bit."

20 THE WAR COUNCIL

All parties were seated at the big "King Arthur" table in MaMere's dining room with the exception of Hawk and the Boggart.

Hawk sent Jada and Justin out on guard duty, so seated at the table were; Joe, Jace (another of Hawks' sons), Jamie, MaMere, Sam, Max, Myself, and some others that Jamie introduced as her cousins, Aundrea and Brianna. Hawk stood over the Boggart who was seated in a small chair in the corner. Everyone stared at him until Hawk said "Ok, spill it or you are a dragon treat."

Boggarts are very human looking from a distance. Except for being on the short side, quite hairy, having beak-like noses and pocked faces from warts and boils that their race is prone to develop. And yes, they have the stereotypical pointy ears, or so I was later told.

The Boggart started crying hysterically. Hawk let him cry for a few minutes without saying a word. Then he turned to Sam and said "He doesn't know anything and is of no use. Do you need salt and pepper and a maybe a little lemon to cover the smell?' Sam smiled and said "No, I'm not picky and I am starting to feel a little light headed anyway" and then her dragon fangs and eyes reappeared. It is a pretty scary sight because the teeth are too big for her human mouth and she began drooling heavily.

The boggart jumped up and shouted "OK! Ok! We got wind that there was a reporter up here that had found where the Balance was. Some frantic woman called a newspaper in Los Angeles about her brother being on a big assignment out here and he had gone missing. Something about not picking up money she wired. The Editor of that newspaper called in a private investigator who in turn called his contact here in Louisiana Brady Bauchan (Brady is the leader of that nasty branch of

Fey this boggart got his orders from as I mentioned earlier.)

When they found out that the reporter was seen leaving with Joe Eschte, they alerted Crowley. (Alan Crowley, leader of the LeFey Cabal – this Cabal is a modern day Witch's Coven/Cult that operates like a Mafia in New Orleans.)

Brady has been watching the Eschte's for a long time waiting for a lead to The Balance. The LeFey Cabal hired an oracle who said that this family would lead us to the Balance. I swear that's all I know, everything, please don't let that thing eat me!"

Jamie whipped around and shouted at MaMere, "How did they know about Dan! How long has he been here?" MaMere calmly replied "He has been here with me for three days." It was my turn to jump up, "That's not true!, I have only been here one day!" MaMere shushed me and told me; "Remember when ya cut yer finger, Chere?" "Yes" I said. "Weeeell, I used a teeny tiny lil bit o yer blood to spell ya and find out de true nature of yo heart.

Dat took me bout two days, you are a very complex young man, yeah and one with a big future too. I put ya back in yo chair when I was done. It might' a jes seemed lahke ya only blinked. Ya actually saw Jamie arrive with the Nereids, but ya just tawt you was daydreaming, yeah." Jamie mumbled "I thought it was a dream too. I was really tired from the ride across the ocean." Then she added more clearly, "I thought you were actin kinda funny rushing me off soon as my foot hit the dock since you were the one who made me rush to the island as fast as possible."

"You put a spell on me!" I shouted. "Impossible, that's just not possible! MaMere laughed and said "Not possible Chere, den what was Jamie wearin when she came outta de water and who was she wit?"

I spluttered, "She... she... was, ok, well she was nude and there were two girls with her but they were silvery, kind of like fish... "MaMere said "Uh huhhh, an ya ever did see girls like dat befor' and where did dey go when dey lef?"

I sat back down mumbling to myself while Jamie sat there still fuming at MaMere for not telling her that he had been here that long (especially since it might have given her time to get to know the man of *her* dreams before the shit hit the fan) or the details of what she found out of him or the danger they were in before now.

Hawk took over the conversation once again and told the boggart he was free to go. The ugly little fairy ran from the house like his pants were on fire. Jamie said, "You think he remembered that Jean is still in the front yard?" Hawk said, "Nope, but Jean is going to make sure he gets back to town... with the proper motivation."

"But what if he tells the others what he saw here tonight?" Jamie asked. Hawk said "I hope he recounts every detail. It will make guarding this place a little easier if they know about our two new recruits."

As soon as he got the words out of his mouth, they heard the blood curdling scream of the Boggart who had indead forgotten what was still lying under the porch.

Sam shouted, "Yeah!, we will eat anything that comes close, our food is coming to us for a change!" Max leaned back in his seat and sat there with his arms crossed, nodding and grinning. Jamie, still angry, looked at Sam and Max and said "Why didn't you shift before, for me?" They looked at each other and Max said, "We weren't sure we could but since you were present when we hatched we sort of imprinted on you and copied some of your memories and abilities." Jamie said, "But if that's the case, I'm not a shifter so you shouldn't have been able to shift if either of you imprinted on me."

Sam replied with a cryptic smile, "Are you sure?" Jamie sat there with her mouth hanging open, the possibility of being able to shift having never occurred to her before.

"So, it comes down to this." Hawk said. "They know about the Balance being here they just don't know that the Balance is the girls or they would have gotten them a long time ago. We have always had the advantage no one knowing exactly what form the Balance took."

Jamie grumbled saying she thought the Fae's and Witches believed it was her and that's why she was always running into trouble.

Hawk gave her a stern look for interrupting him during his briefing, but went on, "Given the isolation of the island, it is only a matter of time before they put two and two together and figure it out. If Brady has sent a spy and the LeFey's are involved you can just bet that they will hit us and hit us hard looking for the Balance. If they get their hands on them it will throw the balance of magic in the world into chaos."

Hawk continued, "We will need to get everyone here, although it is isolated it is still the easiest place to defend and it is away from most humans, eliminating the need for damage control and police interference. However, it also means that we are cut off without an avenue for retreat if we need it."

"My plan is to have the Wolves guard all access points on the mainland. My family and the other Raptors will provide aerial support. I have run drills with them in the past in case this time ever came, so they are familiar with what is expected of them."

"I will patrol this island along with the Dragons making periodic appearances in the air as a show of strength, although we do have a problem with them. It appears that the dragons need a constant source of fuel if they are going to be effective for combat lasting more than 10 minutes...Any suggestions?"

Sam piped up and said "Um, can't we just eat them as we go or are you saving them for dessert?" Hawk looked dumbfounded and said, "Yeah, sure that would solve the problem. So I guess that takes care of that concern along with the prospect of housing for prisoners."

Aundrea pointed out that with diverse cultures that inhabit this island that the care and maintenance of any enemy here would be taken care of in a manner not unlike chumming the water for sharks. (Consequently, that thought still gives me the shivers as I recall this story.)

Seeing me turn a little green at that comment, Hawk gave Aundrea a pointed look and then addressed Sam and Max, "MaMere or I will decide who we keep as captives and only after they have been interrogated will they become anyone's kibble."

Addressing the Dragons, he said, "Given what little we know about you and your abilities, is there anything else that could be of help to us?" Max stated that although they got tired when they were practicing maneuvers, Hawk needed to remember that they had also just flown over from New Zealand without taking a rest. Hawk asked him how long that had taken them and he said we would have been faster, but Sam kept chasing whales and getting off course. He said that it had taken them about a little more than half the day and they took off at in the morning right after the Nereids came to get Jamie.

Hawk did a quick calculation in his head and realized that they had to have been flying at about 610 miles an hour. He looked at them and asked Sam, "Are you sure about those times?"

She said "Yeah, we can go even faster because we don't need oxygen to breath and we can get a good head start and get out of the atmosphere and just practically cruise most of the way, nobody told us we had to get here fast or we would have been here a lot sooner. Jamie just told us to follow her at a distance and not spook the fish girls. Being able to push with your wings helps and if you're weightless, it helps a lot.

Ok, that made more sense, sort of. Feeling a little envious, Hawk went on "Do you have any other abilities, magical... anything?"

Sam said "We are immune to magic if that helps." "We can't be spelled or turned and there is only one way to kill us." Hawk asked "and that would be..."

Sam laughed and Max said "on a need to know basis and no one needs to know but another dragon and they already know."

Hawk defended his question and said "what if there is something that could kill you, how will we protect you." Sam snorted and said "if we tell you then we have to eat you. Dragons are always hungry, do you still want to know?"

Max laughed with her, it must have been an inside joke that no one else got. He also told Hawk that given what they were dealing with here so far there wasn't any way that they could be harmed by magic and when in Dragon form their scales couldn't be penetrated. So there was no danger of being hurt unless they had something big enough to literally rip them to shreds.

To the best of their knowledge, there wasn't anything that big or sharp enough out there.

Watching them in the sky and hearing the bad-assed attitude they were putting out, they might get out of hand and become a liability if they didn't learn to take direction or take another creature for granted. Hawk decided to himself that at some point he was going to have to show them just how sharp his talons were and teach them some manners. He was pretty sure they had never tangled with a pissed off Thunder-Hawk.

Max went on to say that maybe they could be trapped and put in a cage, but they would just melt the bars and they would get free.   Unless, of course as Joe pointed out, the cage that was made of stone such as a cave (we learned later that some of their elders had been caught a few times in a cave).

Sam again laughed and said that most dragons preferred caves because sometimes they get indigestion and caves don't catch fire that easily when they burp.

Technically, they could be imprisoned in a cave, but not for long because they would be able to dig, burn or blast their own way out eventually. It would only serve as a minor delay.She said you know you are close to a dragon's lair first because of the smell of sulfur. Then, as you go deeper to the sleeping chamber you will encounter soot and charring on the walls. She said that the sleeping chamber is always "clean and sparkly".

Hawk asked what she meant about that and she said that with the constant intense heat, minerals in the rock walls of a cave would become crystallized or studded with diamonds and other precious gem and minerals; gold, copper, silver, platinum magnesium and uranium for instance. Therefore it would make their caves "shiny" and oh, bacteria free.

"Hmmph" Max said sounding irritated. "She loves that girly stuff. We never seem to be able to keep a place longer than a couple hundred years because nosy humans want to raid the place."

"If you ask me, you would think they would have some respect for a dude's home, but just as it starts getting good and comfortable, something happens and we have to move.

"We had a really bad time when humans dressed in tin cans and felt like they had something to prove... Always barging in and disturbing my naps. After you smoke a few of them you think they would take a hint and leave us alone. Nooooo, we have to find a new cave, she gets in her nesting phase again and..."

Sam quickly interrupted him and said "this is fun, but unless you guys have any other plans or practice drills for us to learn, we are gonna go hang out with the girls". Sam and Max left to find the girls and Hawk continued with the meeting.

Hawk looked at MaMere and asked, "Is there anything else we need to be concerned about? Do you know what's coming?"

She stood up and said "Chere, ya know I can't change da future by telling ya'll what's comin. De Lord and I made an agreement a long, long time ago dat Ah would never interfere wit human destiny. Ah CAN tell ya that ya'll need your sleep an dat tamorrah is gonna be a busy day, yeah. You gotta get as prepared ya can, so go get some rest, Chere it might be a while fo ya'll get anothuh chance."

Jamie said, "I'll go get the girls and get them ready for bed." I asked MaMere if i could choose a couple of books from her collection for some bedtime reading material. She said "fo you Chere, shore, but don't mess with any a da books on da top shelf, they … are very old and fragile. Jes don't ever read da words out loud. Sometimes de right combination of words has a lot of power.".

21 TAKE US TO YOUR SECRET PLACE PLEASE

Sam and Max left the meeting with the humans to find Jamie's children. The Thunder-Hawk was too suspicious and intelligent. Unlike the humans that their kind had dealt with in the past, this one was a thinker. It wouldn't be long before he would find their weakness. He asked too many pointed questions not to figure it out soon. They weren't familiar enough with human language patterns yet to keep from inadvertently giving themselves away.

They spotted the girls teasing the creatures in the mud pits. The girls would walk near one of those pits and something would pop up and make a grab for them. The girls would move with incredible speed that appeared as if they had disappeared and materialized someplace else. When the creatures missed them repeatedly the bogs began to boil with movement. Small irritated screeching sounds could be heard coming from deep within the ground.

Sam and Max watched them from a distance for a few minutes. Sam looked at Max and said, "The humans don't know what they can do and they have been hiding their abilities well." Max kept watching the girls and said, "Yup, they don't have a clue what they have on their hands." They both stood there in silence for a few minutes more before the girls gave up their game and walked over to Sam and Max as if they knew they had been watching them all along.

Maddey looked at Max and said "Yes, you are right about Hawk he will figure it out soon. Don't worry though he will not exploit his knowledge. He is as old as your race is and knows what it is to protect an ancient race in danger of extinction. No, they don't realize exactly what we are, but they aren't humans either. When the time comes, they will adapt to us as we have to them."

Max gave a quick glance of concern to Sam and turned back to continue listening to the child. "They do love us and will protect us with their lives if they have to. Momma would do it without even thinking, for it is instinctive of her nature and her depth of love for us. We need to leave here to avoid getting her killed trying to defend us. Take us to your secret place please."

Max nodded his agreement and began his change without further comment. When his change was complete, he told Sam, "I will take them both to our home. You can guard my wing until we are clear of danger then circle back and defend the island and Jamie. We owe her a debt for releasing us and giving us more than any other creature has before her. Respect, completely, and without expectations.

Sam nodded and completed her own change, within a minute or so they were airborne. They circled the island once before they flew away and saw the invaders landing on the shore.

Jamie had just stepped out of the house and was searching for the girls. Within minutes she would be attacked. Sam started to make a rescue attempt and Adey yelled, "Wait! She is strong enough and the others are close by. She will be safe for now, we must continue. If we go back, she will die defending us."

Sam looked back at Max and though it was hard because she had established a bond with the human woman, she fell back in line with Max and the girls.

It seemed as though they had been flying forever. For once, the girls were eerily quiet and still and they all continued their flight in silence. As they neared the mountains, Sam spared a moment of concern on whether or not the extreme cold of the altitude would affect the girls. Again, Maddey surprised them again with the completely adult thought pattern cleverly concealed in the child's body and assured them that she and her sister would be fine.

It was as if these children were old spirits that were being incubated in the bodies much like they were incubated in their eggs. Max signaled Sam and told her "I've got this now, go ahead and keep their Mother safe."

"How am I going to explain why we took the girls?" Max gave her a toothy grin and said, "You will think of something. Blame it on me. Old Featherhead already thinks I'm too impetuous, use that."

Sam dipped her wings in response and she pushed hard toward the heavens to reach maximum acceleration. She took off like a Harrier Jet and in seconds and she was gone.

Max continued his flight over the Andes Mountains to their sanctuary. He and Sam had just been there a couple of weeks ago clearing everything out. After all they hadn't checked on it in nearly a thousand years. It wasn't too bad. They just burned out the spider webs and melted the debris that had collected there. It was still amazing to them that with all the technology the humans had developed over the years, the place was still a secret.

After doing a little exploring around, he and Sam did find signs of human habitation. Though the signs were very old, they had apparently been witnessed coming and going at some point during their times of residency. There were hieroglyphic symbols on the walls of some nearby ruins that resembled large flying snakes.

As Max neared the entrance he sent a thought back to the children clinging to his back and let them know he was about to land. Adey thought back at him, "Good thing you had it cleaned. It's not nice bringing guests to a messy lair." Max chuckled the way only a dragon can (snorting) at her blatant knowledge of ... well everything.

When he landed, he changed to human form careful to materialize his pants with him and told them to stay put and he left to gather food and fuel for a fire to keep the children warm. When he returned, they already had a fire and were asleep on a pile blankets that he knew for a fact were not there before.

He approached them to examine their bedding and discovered that they were made of some kind of organic plant materials that smelled like the native plants from this area. He looked hard at them and thought to himself that they couldn't possibly have gathered the fibers and woven them that quickly without the use of some kind of magic. Maddey opened her eyes hearing his thoughts clearly and said to him. "You forget, my Great Winged Serpent King, we are the Balance, That which keeps the Magic in control, in check and out of the hands of humans to be corrupted and used for the ultimate destruction of every living being on this planet. Of course we called our blankets to us."

Max didn't know what to say so he said nothing. He dropped his supplies and lay down in the entrance to the tunnel in the mountain to rest. Before long, he was fast asleep. He dreamed dreams of his and Sam's pasts. He dreamed of the old days and magicians and sorcerers of old. He dreamed of flying high and free with other Dragons before the time of men.

22 ARACHNIA

I was reading some of those old books of MaMere's and stumbled across a Bible. It was a very large book with gilded edges, wonderful illustrations on vellum paper.

I looked a little harder and found that the book was one of the first copies of the Gutenberg Bible. It had to be!

The first printing of the bible was by Johann Gutenberg. Preparation of it probably began soon after 1450, and the first finished copies were available in 1454 or 1455. However, it is not known exactly how long the Bible took to print.

Gutenberg made three significant changes during the printing process. The first sheets were rubricated by being passed twice through the printing press, using black and then red ink. This was soon abandoned, with spaces being left for rubrication to be added by hand.

Sometime later, after more sheets had been printed, the number of lines per page was increased from 40 to 42, presumably to save paper.

Therefore, pages 1 to 9 and pages 256 to 265, presumably the first ones printed, have 40 lines each. Page 10 has 41, and from there on the 42 lines appear. The increase in line number was achieved by decreasing the interline spacing, rather than increasing the printed area of the page.

I know all this because I had to give a dissertation on the subject in college. This copy had 40 lines!!! The book was priceless.

How in the world had the old woman gotten her hands on it? A folded piece of parchment fell out from the middle of the book.

It was a hand-written note that read, "Frau Stella, Vielen Dank für alle ihre Weisheit und Führung. Bitte akzeptieren Sie die erste Kopie unserer bemühen mit meiner dankbarkeit. Johann April 1450"

My German was a little rusty, but I think that it says something to the effect of Thank you for wisdom and guidance.

This couldn't be possible, but if this is correct, then I was holding a first draft worth millions that was given to a woman who's chair I was sitting in more than 561 years ago!

Hell, what am I thinking, I have met Dragons today that were supposed to be mythical creatures and learned that most of the boogeyman stories are real. I seem to keep being shocked and surprised by every new creature I have met since I got here and reminding myself that by now I should be getting used to it after all that I had seen. I had the sinking feeling that my life as I knew it was over.

I must have dozed for a few minutes, because I woke up to having my face wet sanded. Stella's weird cat was sitting on my chest licking the skin off my face. This is the strangest cat I have ever seen. It looks like a normal little calico cat that has been through a paper shredder. It only has patches of hair here and there. It's back end is almost completely bald and sort of red looking like a baboon butt, but it's the eyes that are deeply disturbing.

It has one cute little green cat eye that sort of glows and one human green eyeball in a cat's head. That's a really creepy thing to wake up to. While I was trying to clear my head, I heard a noise outside, kind of a scuffling noise. I put the book back where I found it and was about to go outside, when a bleary-eyed Hawk came running down the hall.

"Did you hear it too?" "Yeah", I replied. We both went outside to the front porch to discover that everything was covered in spider webs. "Dammit! It's Arachnia! She has woven a dream web around us. Go wake the others and get a headcount. Arachnia is a sneaky bitch. You can't hear her coming until she's got you in her web. She must have been here last night spinning. That's why we were all so tired. Come to think of it, why are you still up?"

"I had been dozing actually but Stella told me I could take a look at some of her books. I believe I found the Gutenberg bible and became sort of engrossed."

"That explains it, you were protected from the web's full effects" he said. I asked, "Why, does the book have magical powers too?" Hawk looked at me like I had grown a third head and he said "It's the

Bible man, the written word of God. The first text unpolluted by politics and man's desires. That particular book is the only one in existence. All the other copies were revised and edited by the Pope before publication."

"But in my research, the first Gutenberg is at the Vatican and was reviewed by the Pope." Hawk a little distracted and looking out the windows for signs of movement said, "Trust me, that one is the uncensored version." I replied, "Then how did Stella get it?" Irritated by my distracting questions and rushing out the door, he yelled at me "Look, we don't have time for question and answer right now, son. Let's just say she has had a lot of boyfriends over the years. Now go wake the others like I told you!"

A few minutes later, everyone was at the big table and Hawk came in with Jamie. "I found her cocooned to the big Cypress out back. When she went to find the girls, she discovered Arachnia at work. She watched the dragons take the girls to find a place to hide before she got sprayed with webbing. Has anyone located them yet?"

I told him that the bedrooms were empty and then we all looked at MaMere for an answer. She said, "All Ah can tell ya is dat dey is ok. They went wit da dragons and dey is safe for raht now. We still have ta deal wit dese Rou Garous before we can git de girls back or dey will use Jamie to try an trap them."

"What's a Rou Garou?" I asked. Coughing and coming more fully out of her stupor, Jamie said "It used to be a term that the Cajuns used for a Wolf man or Werewolf. Mothers used to tell small children that if they didn't behave, the Rou Garou or Loup Garou would get them. MaMere just uses it as a slang term for the bad guys. I thought you guys were never gonna figure out we were under attack. What took you so long or was he still playing 21 thousand questions!"

Stella looked at me and patted me on the back and said, "Chere, Ah know ya is new to da goings on of dis world, but can ya save ya questions fa later? A little embarrassed, I mumbled sure just the reporter in me makes me crazy. "It's ok, dat's one a da reasons ya here. Arachnia puts out an airborn venom dat puts her victims into a sleep or trance. Fortunately, we are strong… sometimes her victims sleep raht though bein' eaten."

"Hawk, can ya locate the patrols? Ah can't hear dem anywhere, Chere. My calls are bein blocked again." Hawk looked at Jamie and asked "Can you use your sight now?" She looked at him and said "yeah, but I'm fuzzy and can't focus."

MaMere said "Jamie come sit here at de table, you too Dan." We moved to the big round table and she instructed Jamie and I to hold hands. "Now, Ah know dis is hard fo ya, but Dan you gonna have to clear yo mind and focus on Jamie. Try to help her see."

I really had no clue how I was going to help Jamie see, but I did as MaMere instructed and cleared my head. I closed my eyes and focused on Jamie. I could see her in my mind's eye and it was like I was looking out a dirty window. I imagined taking my hand and wiping the window clean.

Suddenly, Jamie said "There they are! Jada is circling the island screeching, Jean is fighting with something in the water and Joe and Jace are in a pirogue trying to find a way in to us."

"I am also getting a clear message from the girls and Sam and Max. Sam and Max have taken them to their place of protection. Sam says that nothing has ever been able to breach their barriers and survive the experience. They must have had to do a little digging to find it after all this time. I'm surprised that it was still there. After all the world has changed a lot since Dragons roamed."

"Wow, that was amazing, I could see and hear everything she could. I felt a pull from deep inside my gut when I felt her reach for power and my heart was beating really fast. I realized I was looking inside Jamie as well. I had flashing images of flying with big wings and running through the trees with big strong paws? I have never experienced anything like it. I fed the information to MaMere and watched as her eyes widened a little and she said, "Chere, you can see ahead of you. Be careful, Mon Amie."

I told MaMere, "The moment I took her hands I started feeling kind of tingly and the more I focused the stronger the feeling got. I was becoming more and more confused because I began trying to see more of things I didn't understand."

Jamie said "It was the same for me. The moment I took his hands, I felt a power surge. I know the dragons are very far away, but I normally can only get impressions of feeling from that far away, this was a very clear dialog. YOU are the empath that Hawk and Jean have detected on this island!"

Stella chuckled and looked at her and said "Ah was wonderin when ya would make da connection of where de power was comin from. Ah tol ya Chere, you two complement each other. Like you, Dan is an Empath, but of a different kind dat is almost parasitic. Meaning dat he can adopt or share de powers of others and den amplify dem to suit his needs, he is one of US."

Now that I was starting to get the message, I wouldn't have believed it if I hadn't actually experienced it. I also had a feeling that I have known Jamie for a long time. I got that feeling when I first saw her. Now that I think about it, she was always the female in all my dreams for as long as I can remember.

Jamie leaned over and squeezed my hand, "Well you can stop blushing Dan. Remember I can hear your thoughts too. MaMere always told me that there was someone out there for me. I wasn't sure what she meant about that, but when I first saw you, I recognized you too. But right now we have bigger things to think about and we need to get moving."

Before we left, I asked MaMere if she knew how many supernatural creatures there were in the world and she said, "Chere, ya might as well ask me how many stars dere are in de sky yeah."

When I just stood there and continued to watch her she continued, "Dan, dere are many many races dat humans don't have a clue dey co-exist wit.

"Some interact wit humans on a regular basis, so dey is de ones dat are the stuff of de bedtime stories and old tales passed down from generation ta generation. But dere is also many of dem dat never have to make any contact wit de human race and are only found out if ya have done something to make dem really mad or encroach on what dey believe is dere homes."

Hawk got us moving again and said "Everyone get some machete's from MaMere and any other weapons you might need. Jada says that there is large party moving toward us and Jean and the others won't last long without help. Dan, you did say you could fight didn't you?"

"Yeah, I can fight, but I am not superhuman like you guys. I am good with a broadsword though, I kind of went through a Conan phase in college and discovered it was a great stamina builder. I still train with them, will that be enough?"

Hawk smiled "More than enough, every little bit helps, most of these creatures can't be killed with just a gun. You will get used to combat, just stick close to Jamie. She usually has a way of finding trouble, you can have her back."

Jamie said, "Come with me Conan Dan, and by the way Hawk, I resent that last remark. Trouble usually finds me and I just deal with it."

Hawk pointed to the swamps and said "there are three pirogues on the bank there, you two head that way and take them out. Be careful, some of them may be our allies, so don't go in with the kill first ask questions later method. Use your knives to clear your way. I am going to the front and try to get in the air so I can relieve Jada."

"MaMere, can you reach the other troops and call them in?" MaMere answered Hawk, "Ah already did Chere, but Ah'm havin trouble getting tru to dem. Someone will have to go git dem." Now, Ah need to cook me up a lil batch of Insecticide to take care of a long lost friend who forgot her manners.".

23 DEAD STAYS DEAD

I asked why we were using knives and machetes and Jamie explained because they were the most versatile weapons, lightweight and easy to handle with an edge that can slice through bone.

She reiterated what Hawk said; "that some of these things can't be killed with bullets unless you blow their heads off. A machete, knife, sword or broad-axe will cut off a head lickety-split and you don't have to worry about them healing themselves and catching you with your back turned."

"Without a head, dead stays dead. Fire works pretty good too, but sometimes it takes too long and you have to make sure it burns to nothing but ashes and then scatter them completely."

I didn't even want to think about it too long because I was afraid I would regain my senses and run screaming all the way back to Los Angeles. Lord, how I missed L.A., all nice and calm with your everyday regular crimes. All a mugger wanted was your wallet.

Jamie went to what looked like a tool shed behind the house and grabbed a crossbow, (a large knife that didn't look anything like machete) for herself and a 357 Magnum. Some toolshed she had, more like a private armory. I told Jamie "I thought you said blades were better."

She laughed and replied "I said you had to take the heads off. This little thing will do that quite well. Besides, like Hawk said; every little bit helps." She turned to me and said "help yourself".

I saw a collection of the crude machete's and several other weapons that didn't quite appeal to me when I saw standing in the corner was a pair of swords.

I grabbed them and started strapping them on when Jamie said with a smirk, "You know, a machete is a lighter weapon and easier for someone not used to combat to start out with".

I stood up and looked her right in the eye and replied "I told you I have had a little training". She shrugged and walked away "Ok Dan-O it's your funeral, just don't get in my way, because if you do I will kill you myself".

MaMere came out to say something to Jamie and stopped speaking to stare at me and my swords. "Excellent choice Chere, dey look good on you." Then she looked around and spotted the cat sitting in the corner of the shed. "Scratchy, Mes Amie, what'cha got up yer little claws, you."

The cat just blinked and twitched her whiskers or what was left of them and ambled away. "Anyway, I was jest makin sure ya had what ya needed. Now I got to git to work mahsef."

We started running down the path to the swamp when I heard a strange chirping sound and Jamie hissed a warning to get down.

We dropped to the ground just in time to miss being seen by 4 large spiders that stood almost 3 feet tall, these things were huge! We waited for them to pass by us and then we inched our way up to our feet.

Jamie looked all around us and whispered to me and said "Watch out, they have spun trip wires all over the place. We are in the middle of a giant spider web". I took my swords in hand and Jamie used the machete to cut the fine threads that might announce our position as we moved forward.

We got just out of site of the house when we were suddenly surrounded by more of the spiders. Jamie and I instinctively turned back to back and faced outward. Jamie yelled "Watch your eyes, they can spit venom and blind you!"

Fantastic, things just keep getting better and better. One of the spiders jumped toward Jamie and she sliced its abdomen in half cleanly then they all attacked at once.

I didn't think, I just moved. I swung my swords like helicopter blades. I don't know where it came from, but I was moving faster than I have ever moved. I felt like I was getting a supernatural adrenaline push from somewhere. Green and yellow goo was flying everywhere.

Terrified into action, my only thought was to block their attacks. With sweeping circular movements in front of my body, I defended myself as I had spent so many years training to do. Bridging my sword above my head to my forearm to create a shield for my head from aerial attacks and making sweeping movements crossing my chest, I cut and sliced anything that came at me. Jamie and I moved in a tandem, attacking and defending me with my swords and her with her crossbow and machete in the same fashion. It was as if we had fought together all our lives.

It was all over in a matter of seconds, but it felt like an eternity. Just as we were catching our breaths, we heard a chorus of screeching. Suddenly all the trees and ground looked like it was being coated in an avalanche of spiders. Jamie yelled, "Run!" We took off down the trail to the other side of the swamp.

Jamie yelled again as we were running, "Don't step off of the trail! There are bogs that are the same as quicksand and there are things that MaMere has living down there in the bottom of them. They will eat anything that lands close to their holes."

Just as she said that I heard a loud screeching and splashing one of the spiders that was coming at us from our rear flank must have found a pit. One moment it was running toward us and then it sank a little in the grass and mud and then something popped up out of the ooze and yanked it completely beneath the surface.

I guess I had stopped and was staring when I saw that thing in the bog grab the spider. "Keep moving!" Jamie screamed at me. She didn't have to tell me twice because I had already started running again, after having seen how quick the spider was taken, I wasn't going to hang around and be next on the menu.

Jamie looked up and still running, she grabbed the crossbow in one hand and nailed a spider that was dropping down on us from the tree branches above us and nailed ripped another in two with her machete in the other hand, never missing a step, a regular Annie Oakley.

We came to a sharp bend in the trail and were surrounded again. We were fighting furiously, but they kept coming we were being overrun. Jamie had a long gash across her chest and my arms were burning from the strain.

I was covered in cuts and scratches. I guess one of the spiders had bitten or cut into my left shoulder because I had blood running down my arm making my grip on the sword a little slippery. I didn't know how much longer we could fend them off when there was a roar from above and fire from the sky came raining down all around us.

We looked up and a dragon was circling us turning the spiders into crispy critters and the webbing into something like burned burnt cotton candy. The dragon landed and gobbled the spiders down as soon as they attacked. Funny how they sounded like someone eating potato chips the way they crunched when the dragon munched them down.

When they were all consumed Sam changed back to a human, this time with clothes. Jamie, panting hard and trying to catch her breath said "Thanks, you came just in time, where's Max?" Sam said "we did rock, paper, scissors and he had to stay and babysit. He's still screaming that I cheated."

Jamie looked at Sam and said Did you? "Of course", she answered with a grin. "Look, I can get back in the air and give Hawk and Jada some help, but I've been melting the webbing everywhere and the spiders just spin more, faster than I can melt it without burning the whole island to the ground."

"The biggest concentration is in the direction you are headed. I'll come with you to try to attack from the ground to get to the Mama spider so we can make some headway, Ok? I will lead the way, let's go!"

Sam changed back to her dragon and started running. I can't tell you how relieved I felt running next to a fire breathing dragon. I can't believe I just said that or that I was actually able to keep up with her pace. Oh, well, que surah que surah. My life will never be the same again.

As we ran, the webs got thicker and stronger. We were almost to the other side of the swamp when we ran into the center of the mass of webs. It was so thick it actually shut out all natural light and we were encased in walls of web. We looked up and saw one of the largest spiders I could imagine just above us.

Just as Sam the dragon was about to spit fire, the spider shot a web at her muzzle and glued it shut. In the next second it shot several more times and had the dragon pinned and cocooned in webbing. I ran to Sam and tried to cut some of the webs loose when it shot me with webbing and I was stuck to the dragon as well.

Jamie started firing off bolts from her crossbow, but they just bounced off. She dodged a shot of webbing by somersaulting in the air and coming down next to the spider who was now on the ground. She struck with her machete/bowie knife, but it couldn't penetrate the big spiders' tough hide.

Jamie ran and dodged several more times until she was close to me she grabbed one of the swords that I had dropped and turned to face the spider. This was the first time I got a good look at it. It had an almost human head, but with 3 pairs of large eyes on its forehead, no nose and huge fangs in its mouth.

It screamed in a high pitched, earsplitting screech "Wheeerrre iiiisss the Baaallannnnccce!" Giiiivvve meeee theeee baaalannnccce annnd III wiiill leeet yoou lllllvvvvve"!

Jamie laughed and screamed back "The Balance is mine Bitch, and I will never give it to an overgrown bug!"

"IIII aaaammm Queeeeeen Arrrrachnnnniaaaa! IIIII wwwiiill suuuck theee liiiife ouuut of yooourrrr petsssss whiiiile yooou waaaatch, tiiiiny huuuummmannn."

Jamie yelled, "I may be small, but I am NOT HUMAN, you go back to the hell you came from!" Jamie attacked running for the underside of her abdomen sliding like a base runner stealing home plate.

The spider skittered around and started stabbing at Jamie with some kind of stinger attached to the end of her tail.

Jamie moved fast and stabbed up with the sword to impale the spider in the vulnerable abdomen but she wasn't fast enough because just as she stabbed, the stinger hit her in the back. While I looked like Jamie had scored a good strike it was just not deep enough to kill the spider. Jamie dropped to the ground. She just laid there and didn't move.

All the while, I had been sawing at the webs with my other sword until I had one arm free. I'd started working on Sam's bindings when the spider nailed me in my free arm with her stinger as well. It felt like she tore my arm off, but when I opened my eyes and peeked a look, it was still there.

Then my entire body felt like it was on fire from the inside, I could actually hear the poison making its' way though my veins with a roaring sound. The spider stabbed at Sam too, but she couldn't seem pierce Sam's scales. With Sam's snout tied shut with webbing, all she could was twitch and jerk and let out was puffs of smoke.

It kept stabbing looking for a weak spot. Sam was roaring and trying to thrash out of the webs. The harder she thrashed the giant spider would splatter us both with more web.

I guess her venom started affecting my brain just about then because my vision got kind of fuzzy and I felt like I was transported back in time... waaay back in time.

24 IN THE FLESH

I saw two beautiful women dressed like
Amazon or Greek Warriors and they were
fighting side by side against an opposing
force and running up the side of a
mountain.

They came to a cave and ran inside.
"This must be it!" one of them yelled at the
other. Inside the cave was a long chest.
The smaller woman told the other, "Break
open the chest and get the Trident and
take it back to Poseidon! I will hold them
off while you open it!"

I couldn't see her face because the
vision was coming from behind her. The
other woman took her sword and bashed
the lock on the chest and opened it.

As she looked inside, a maniacal expression came over her face and she screamed "Finally! It's Mine! Now I will be able to defeat you all and you will all bow to me! I will never have to do your bidding or listen to your incessant wining about your struggle over humans and your new found morality!" she shrieked.

The other woman turned slowly around and said sadly, "You would betray me by stealing Poseidon's Trident that was left in my safekeeping? Somehow, I thought that your story of being overwhelmed and forced to give up the location sounded a little weak especially for a warrior of your experience. After seeing you fight in battle, I had a hard time believing that one, but you were my most trusted friend... a sister to me. What reason did I have to think that you would betray me."

Before the woman standing over the chest could reach in and claim her prize the woman at the entrance to the cave raised her sword and blasted her with pure energy. "Warrior you may be, but I'm still a Goddess lest you forget." She shook her head and said sadly; "Arianna, my closest friend and confidant, the one whom I held with the deepest affection. For your greed and betrayal, you will get your wish to become the most powerful being in your domain. However, since you choose to have no more morals or loyalty than an insect, you shall have domain over the bugs of this world."

When the smoke cleared, I could see that the other woman raised her head from the ground and it was the giant spider lady that was currently kicking our asses.

Then I heard Jamie in my head. She was weak, but alive. Thank God! She told me to fight the neurotoxins with the power of my mind and try to get free. She poured all her mental strength into me and I started moving my arm again to continue cutting through the web.

I was just about to cut through the binding on Sam's muzzle when the spider plastered again me with another coat of web putting an end to all movement on my part.

"NNooowww IIII willlllllll draaaaaain yoooou unnnntilllll yoooou giiiive me the baaalannnnce or diiiiiie" it screeched. It reared up and was about to bite Jamie with its' maw of fangs when with a little short pop and the smell of burnt ozone a woman appeared out of nowhere.

She resembled MaMere, a much younger version, she could have been her granddaughter, the similarity was so strong.

She was beautiful with long flowing black hair that ran down her back to the ground. She was dressed in a Roman or maybe Greek armor, complete with gold leg shields, chest plate and gauntlets.

She looked like she stepped right out of time itself. She looked just like the woman who turned the other woman into the Spider Lady from my vision. She was holding a gold spear in her hand that looked vaguely familiar.

The spider backed up and screeched "Teetthhyyyyyssss"! IIII thhhought yoooou had ffffaded awaaaay with the ottther Tiiitaaans"!!!

Tethys bowed and said "In the flesh, the others faded because humans quit needing them. The nature of Motherhood never ends and so I will never end. I am as strong as I ever was."

"Thhheee Onnne Gooddd fffforrrbbbbidddsss wwwwoorrsssshiippp ooofff allll ooooothhherrrs, wwwwhhhhhyyyy hhhhaaasss hhhheee aaallllooowwweeddd

yyyyooouuuu tttoooo
rrreeemmmaaaiiinnn?"

"Stupid Spider, do you not realize the source of all power? My power is His to Control and direct for the good of Human Kind as it has always been. We, as magical entities only came into existence during his time of rest which lasted a Millennia."

During that time, many of his children forgot him in his slumber and began to dream of other Gods that would serve their childish desires. When he woke, although he was jealous and angry at what his children had done, he continued to give them his love and still granted them the will to choose in the end. I don't need to be worshipped or given sacrifices of any kind so I was not banished to another world or imprisoned like the others. My strongest gift is of love, so we sort of made a deal and I serve Him with my abilities. What's your excuse?

"IIIII haaavvveee hhaaaadddd tooo hhhhiiiiddddeee mmmmyyyy trrruuueee fffooorrrmmmm foorrrr eeeoooonnnnns thhhheeee foooorrmmm yyyyooouuu currrrssssseddd mmmmeee wiiiithhhhhh, wwwwaaaiiiitttiiinngg fffooorrr thheee

chhhaaannnncccccceee toooo
reeettttuuurrnn toooo poooooowweerrrrr."

Thhhheee baaaalllllaaaannnnccce
wwwiillll ggggiiiivvveee mmmmeee
mmmmyy poooowwwweeerrr baaaccckkk.
Giiiivveeee ttthhhheeemmmm tttooo
mmeeee noooowwwww!!

Tethys calmly said "I don't think so.
God gave them to me to watch over.
Besides, they are my grandbabies and NO
ONE touches my grandbabies!!!"

Then there was a blur of movement and
Tethys had the spider writhing on the end
of her spear like a giant crab. While they
were talking, Tethys had been moving into
position distracting the spider with their
conversation.

Tethys shifted the spear in her hand
and faster than you could blink an eye, had
the spider pinned on the ground with a
loud ground shaking thump. "Now I will
treat you like the insect you have always
been." She took arrows from the quiver on
her back and with inhuman thrusts and
incredible speed, she pinned each one of
the spider legs to the earth with an arrow
in each joint and in its' abdomen just like a
scientific specimen.

"You will remain here where I can keep an eye on you for all time." Tethys magically produced a small vial of green liquid and poured it down the spider's throat. The spider turned brown and dried up instantly.

All that was left was Stella's weird cat in a digging frenzy trying to bury the exoskeleton as if it was a deposit in her litter box.

25 SHE'S A GODDESS!

Tethys turned and walked over to Jamie. She put her hand on the wound in Jamie's back and said "Wake up Chere, there is work to be done."

What the HELLL!!! Tethys was MaMere!!! Tethys was a Titan! She's a Goddess!!! I groaned, half afraid, half mad that she tricked me, and also in awe of the fact that she was an actual Goddess.

Jamie stirred and Tethys helped her get to her feet. Jamie said "Thanks, I called and called to you but you didn't answer. I was afraid something had happened to you." Tethys said "Ah was a lil busy, Chere. Ah tol you Ah had to make some bug spray. Now let's get our friends here untangled."

Tethys walked over to us and waved her hand and the webs started melting away. She reached down and grabbed my hand and instantly the pain went away.

She told me that there might be a little mark on my arm where the spider woman stung me, but that from now on, no other poison would affect me unless it was a stronger dose than Arachnia's venom of which there are only a very few creatures on this earth that produce a venom that are its equal. Cool... I think.

Tethys waved her hand again and all the other webbing began melting away as well. She turned to Jamie and said, "We still have work to do. Arachnia wasn't the only supernatural creature involved in the invasion. You two need to get to the pirogues and get help from the mainland. I will work with Hawk and make sure the island is secure. We cannot let them take over the island. There are things here other than the girls that they must never get their hands on." Jamie looked worried, "Just what sort of things?"

"I am a Goddess, the last of the Titans. Do you really think that I would just sit back and let all those magical items be lost for eternity?"

Suspicious, Jamie said "What kind of items are we talking about?" Tethys shrugged nonchalantly and said, "Oh, just Zeus's Bolt, Poseidon's Trident, some golden apples, a little wooden cup, and things of that sort." She put her finger to her chin thoughtfully and added, "Then again, Jean has a few interesting items here that he has also intercepted in the past. Scratchy Patchy keeps track of them for me. She's what you might say OCD with things like that."

I looked at both of them and said "So what you are saying is that this little island of yours holds the treasures both of this world and that of the ancient Gods? Tethys smiled, slipping back to the Cajun dialect again, "Yup, thas about right."

Jamie looked at me and said "most of those things wield incredible power and are as important as my girls in the grand scheme of things. MaMere... uh Tethys, is that why you assume your disguise?"

She looked at Jamie and said "Honey, do you think it would have been easy for you to cuddle up to an old woman or try to snuggle up to me in this form and tell me all your troubles?   Besides, this is not my true form, only one of many."

Jamie pointed to her spear and asked so what's with the big spear, kind of old fashioned don't you think? Tethys chuckled and said "I got this little poker from a nice Italian boy a long time ago."

Examining it I said, "That really doesn't look like an Italian design, perhaps you are mistaken."

"Weell, it's been so long ago, mah sense o' time runs together. I call dem all Italians now, but back den this young man was called a Roman. Dis spear, it didn't really serve him very well… at least not after de Crucifixion and all, but it works fo me just fine." With that she changed back into MaMere.

Her spear became the beautifully carved cane and her body softened into the comforting curves of an old woman. Her eyes twinkled and she said "Some-times it don' pay to call attention to ya sef. Too much work always putting up protective shields an all, takes a lot of energy, yeah" and then she was gone. Poof.

26 YOU'RE NOT AFRAID OF HEIGHTS ARE YOU?

Jamie asked Sam how she was feeling. Sam said "I think I burned my tongue." Jamie also asked her "Can you fly with both of us?"

Sam looked at us and said "Are you kidding? Of course I can, my grandmother once picked up a ship that was adrift on the currents and put it on top of a mountain sticking out of the ocean during a great flood."

She eyed me warily and said, "but one of you will have to ride on my back while I carry the other in my claws. Picking inanimate things up is one thing riding and remaining stable while flying is another."

Jamie looked at me and said "You can carry him in your claws, I won't fall off your back or pinch your wings. Besides, I need to have my hands free so I can use my crossbow if I need to." They both looked at me and Jamie asked "You are not afraid of heights are you?"

Even if I was, I wouldn't have told them. Jeeze, just because a guy is a scholar doesn't mean that he's a wuss. I bet they don't treat Hawk like a pansy. I thought I held my own pretty well fighting the spiders... till I got plastered to the side of a dragon.

Sam said that she needed a bite to eat first and she would be right back. She changed back to her dragon and flew off. While we waited for her to come back, I asked Jamie why didn't Sam just change when she was stuck in the webbing.

Jamie said that she called to her to try that very thing, but she was so mad she couldn't get calm down enough to concentrate on the change. She said to remember, her natural form is a dragon. Changing into a human form takes a lot of power and concentration.

Sam came flying back and with a big toothy dragon smile and thought at us that there was a group of Witches just beyond the trees that were trying to conjure up a spell. She just grabbed one of them as a snack and came rushing back to get us.

Jamie climbed up on her back and got into position. Sam told me to just stand still and she would grab onto the harness for my swords. That way I could have my hands free as well and I could squirm all I wanted to.

When we lifted off I was sure I left my stomach and lower intestines on the ground. There is no roller coaster or amusement park ride that will give you that kind of feeling. We flew straight up and made a big circle around the island.

When I gathered the courage to look down and I had only a moment of panic. Sam's grip on my harness was strong enough that I didn't feel scared. What a freakin' rush!

We found the group of witches and started to swoop down on them, but as soon as we got close, it was like hitting a wall. They had erected some kind of bubble or protective force field dome around themselves.

I thought at Sam, "I thought you were immune to magic." She said, "I said it can't affect me, I didn't say it doesn't work for them."

I still didn't get it when Jamie yelled down at me, "Dragons can't be spelled, but a protective circle will definitely keep them out. The good thing is that it also keeps the witches in so they won't be going anywhere soon."

Jamie said to us in mine and Sam's heads, "let's go check out what else is going on, maybe we can come back with more help and deal with them then."

We circled the island again and found Jean Lafitte ramming some small boats filled with some other creatures. Jamie let me know that they were Trolls.

She was telling me to get into position to fight them when Sam said she had a better idea. Sam said to take a deep breath and hoped I didn't mind getting a little damp.

She made a diving run right at their boat. We narrowly missed the boat and hit the water so hard that it knocked the breath that I had just sucked in right out of me.

We dove down and then came up beside Jean Lafitte. Jamie yelled for me to let go and hang onto the alligator. What the hell, I was NOT going to hang onto an alligator!

At that moment I realized we were being fired on with arrows and guns by the Trolls' boat. Jean dove under and came up under me so that I had no choice but to ride on his back.

He swam away from the battle and Jamie fired her crossbow from Sam's back. Sam blasted the boat with her built in flamethrower breath, but they wouldn't burn. Their boat did but they didn't.

Jamie yelled at Sam, "They're Trolls they don't burn!" Sam dove again and came up under their boat capsizing them. Jamie communicated to me that Trolls were poor swimmers, but could walk on the bottom like a hippo. Once the boat was sunk Jamie dismounted and Jean dove leaving me treading water since we stopped being fired on. I think both Jean and Sam went under for a Troll snack.

After a few minutes some rather large green bubbles surfaced all around us and then Sam surfaced and Jean did too.

Sam said she counted nine in the boat before it sank. Jean said that he sank two other boats before we showed up, but that was the largest boat. He hadn't had a chance to get to any of them before, so he deduced that some of them had gotten away.

27 A CERTAIN AESOP'S FABLE COMES TO MIND

Jean was going to shore to see if he could pick them off from there. He turned to me and grinned a big toothy grin and asked me if I wanted to hitch a ride. A certain Aesop's Fable came to mind, but I shrugged and said why not?

He told me to hop on and we took off heading for shore (When he wanted to be, the old gator was as fast as a boat with a motor. Being as large as he was, it didn't surprise me at all.) Jamie climbed back up on Sam and they told us they were going to see if they could spot any of them from the air.

It was weird being able to communicate with the alligator. In my head he had a distinctly French accent. Not like the Cajuns, but from France, French. His voice was kind of deep and velvety sounding. I think I kind of liked the old pirate, er alligator.

As we swam, I told him that I actually enjoyed swimming and had been a competitive swimmer growing up. He told me that if I spent more time here that he wouldn't mind a little company now and then. I guess it was nice for him to be able to communicate with someone for a change, and I told him so. He said that the only person until recently that had spoken to him since he was changed was Stella. Jamie had never tried to talk to him in his head just at him when she was giving instructions or conveying a message from MaMere. She never listened for any of his responses, so yes, it was nice to have someone else to talk to and he would enjoy doing so when we could have a nice long chat while we weren't at war.

I asked him if he knew who Stella really was. He said yes, he knew she was Tethys, MaMere and a couple of others, but she would always be Stella to him.

I told him that I could tell that he loved her by the way he spoke about her. He said yes, but that she constantly drove him crazy.

I asked about the man on Marie's Birth Certificate, Claude. He chuckled and said there was never anyone named Claude and that he had only been given a reprieve once from his gator sentence and that was to go to the Courthouse and sign Marie's Birth Certificate.

He also said he knew she could change forms and was always afraid that she would find someone else. He said there would never be anyone else for him but her.

I asked him if he was mad at her for changing him. He said yes, but after the first fifty years, he realized that as a normal human, he would have died a long time ago.

In this form, he would be able to be with her as long as he was spelled. The spell kept him in a sort of suspended animation.

I asked if he was jealous of me. He said no, but just don't go giving her kisses. I was reminded of what happened with Hawk.

As we neared shore, we spotted one of the Trolls coming to shore. Jean told me to hang on until we were really close and that he would get his legs and told me to attack his head. He told me that I would have to cut the head off to kill it. After all I had seen and done since I came to this place, I didn't hesitate but answered, I'm game.

I hunkered down a little tighter to the gator to make us more streamlined so as not to make noise and alert the Troll. Even though he was making enough noise he probably couldn't hear us over his own snorting and coughing and splashing.

We moved with surprising stealth and got so close Jean's nose was almost touching him. Jean said "On three, one, two, and on three I jumped up, adrenaline surging through me, I was buzzing with energy and I swung my sword with everything I had and cleaved his head almost off.

The Troll managed to roar in agony with the strike to his head and when Jean bit down on his thigh and took him down, I took the opportunity and swung one more time and the head came off.

The Troll's blood was green. No wonder I hadn't seen red blood in the bubbles earlier...eewwww I had been surrounded in those bubbles! Jean dragged the body a little ways off and came back to me.

We walked a little further together on down the shoreline when we came on another one. This time the Troll got the drop on us.

I guess he didn't spot the 30 foot alligator strolling along beside me or didn't see it as a threat, but it went for me first and grabbed me in a bear hug that threatened to break my ribs.

I gave the head butt that you see in the movies, but it had absolutely no effect, Trolls have hard heads too.   I resorted to my martial arts training and brought my knee up and slammed the heel of my foot with everything I had into the inside of his kneecap. I heard and felt that satisfying crrraaackk! That had him stumbling and broke his hold and I stumbled free.

Then Jean got him by the leg and started thrashing him like a dog with a chew toy. (not an easy feat because this Troll easily made two of me in height alone... just what you would imagine a Troll to be, a walking Dump truck).

Jean stopped long enough for me to chop the head off and thrashed him a few more times for good measure. Two down and eight more to go.

We walked into the underbrush for a little ways and heard noises like something big moving around, we had spotted the rest of the missing Trolls.

Correction, did I say eight more, we discovered a large war party of Trolls. We again went into our diversion tactic of using Jean as an ambush weapon.

I walked right up to them swords drawn and said in my best Clint Eastwood imitation, "You want a piece of me punks?" As expected, they all faced me and began circling. After fighting off the spiders, I began to feel the familiar surge of energy as before. I wasn't sure if it was my own adrenaline fueled fear or some kind of power surge, but I went into Lawn Mower mode.

Circling my body in a facsimile of a Kali fighting defense, I didn't leave them any opening. They couldn't even get close enough to me to do any serious damage. As I swung, my body hummed with the energy and strength.

I was amazed at myself. It felt fluid, like a dance, a deadly dance. As I moved, a strange calm settled in me and I acknowledged that I had made up my mind. I was going to do damage, I was going to kill anything that came at me before they killed me.

Strange, how that feels. I turned and stepped to the side and back of one Troll slicing the achilles tendon and the carotid artery in his neck, as his green smelly blood spurted from him and before his body hit the ground, I was already moving in on the next one. Out of my peripheral vision, I saw Jean finish him off clamping down on the head.

The next charging Troll was mortally wounded with twisting stab to the axillary artery in the armpit and a vicious slice to his gut and forearm cutting the tendons rendering the other hand completely useless on the down-stroke. They might not die right away being Trolls, but they weren't going to inflict any more harm on me right away.

I sliced, stabbed, crushed but I didn't feel anything, I just danced. The only hindrance that I acknowledged was that the grip on my swords was almost slippery due to the amount of gore I was drenched in. I felt like I had risen out of my body and was watching myself in slow motion. It was beautiful and terrifying.

I took my share of blows and had sustained a large gash in my back, and I think my nose was broken, but I couldn't feel it and I vaguely remember seeing stars for a moment. I just spit the blood back at my attacker and jumped up and cut his head off bringing both swords up and striking downward in a V to have the blades meet in his chest.

I just listened to the sounds of destruction, their destruction. The sucking sound the lungs make when they are punctured, the crunching sound skulls make when they are smashed with the hilt of the sword, the popping of muscles from bone when you release them from their roots. I felt fantastic!

As I kept them busy with my little show, I noticed that one by one a Troll would be snatched and dragged away. Their numbers beginning to seriously diminish, the Trolls started to realize what was happening and began to start guarding their own backs. Jean came out of the undergrowth and the site of him shocked even me. He was also covered in green gore, giving a roaring alligator hiss and revealing his huge muzzle of dagger like teeth.

If I haven't conveyed to you before just how big he is, it might help to compare him to being as wide as an economy car and twice the length of two pickup trucks parked end to end. His mouth was about like opening the hood of the car but instead of engine you have six inch teeth...Lots and Lots of teeth.

Anyway, the Trolls now began to defend themselves. They weren't brilliant strategists and relied on the fact that almost nothing could hurt them. Nothing, that is, that wasn't sharp like whirling swords or teeth. They fought and charged like the brutes they were. (As a side note, I found out why they don't burn. Their body mass is simply too dense in more ways than one. No wonder they were hard to kill.)

I have dealt with humans that were like this before. They were so sure of their size and strength now and they really didn't know how to defend themselves effectively. I jumped up and got a Troll by the head in a scissor lock and rolled him to the ground and before he could get his footing, I hacked his head off. Jean simply started eating another, the last two gave up and ran back to the water and didn't stop when they got there. The entire area stank with dead Trolls. Now breathless, I wondered what had happened to Jamie and Sam.

28 HELL STORM

When Jamie and Sam got in the air, they saw Hawk swooping down to the group of witches they had spotted earlier.

After a quick scan of the shore where Dan and Jean had come out the water at and she saw how they worked together to kill the two Trolls, her estimation of Dan's worth went up a notch or two.

The man definitely wasn't a wuss after all and he could handle himself well in combat. She should know, Trolls were hard to kill.

She told Sam to take her back to the Witches. When they got there, Hawk was standing just outside their circle and trying to find a weak spot. She saw the worried look on his face.

"What's the matter?" He looked at her and said "I think we're too late, they have completed the spell." Jamie asked him, "What kind of spell was it?" Hawk shook his head and said, "I got here too late and wasn't able to catch it, but they have called forth something from Hell and they sacrificed one of their own to do it."

Jamie turned to Sam and asked "What was the Witch doing before you ate her?" Sam gave a mental shrug and sent Jamie a memory of what happened. Jamie paled and turned back to Hawk and said "The smell of blood is what attracted Sam. The woman was lying on the rocks; she must have been their sacrifice."

Hawk ran his hand through his hair, "And Sam gobbled her up. The violence of her death strengthened their spell. Otherwise, this weak bunch of Wanna-be Wiccan hacks would have never been able to pull it off. They have called something having to do with the darkness of hell. Whatever they have done, they will never be able to control it they don't have enough power."

Jamie jumped back onto Sam's back and said, "I'm going to get MaMere, she has enough power to send it back." Suddenly the sky started getting dark as if a giant storm was brewing and was concentrated only on the island. The wind started howling, really howling like something alive.

Hawk shouted at them "Go! Before it's too late! Even I can't fly in this!" Sam snorted and jumped into the air like it was nothing to her. It was rough going for Jamie to hold tight, but Sam was strong and well fed.

They flew up and up and up until they flew above the storm. When Jamie looked down she realized what it was they had conjured, the actual Darkness of Hell. Without protection from its storms everyone and everything on the island would die. The very atmosphere fed on souls.

They flew to where she thought MaMere's house should have been but it was so stormy and dark they couldn't see the house from the air. They dove back down into the storm to get to the house.

MaMere was on the front porch waving to her. When they landed she ran to Jamie and told her to get everyone and get them to the house any way she could, it was the only thing that would protect them. She said she would do everything she could to hold back the storm long enough to get everyone here. Jamie immediately used her telepathic powers to talk to everyone she could to tell them what MaMere said.

Hawk responded and said that he could make it on foot and would come through the swamp trail. Dan reported that Jean would take him through the underground stream that fed fresh water to the house.

Joe, Jace, Aundrea and Jada were still on the West side of the island. Jada and Justin would never be able to fly through those winds, but Joe, Jace and Aundrea said they would get Jada to the house, but they were still battling a group of boggarts and werewolves and might need some help with them.

Jamie gave Sam the instructions and off they went to help get the rest of them to the house. When they got to them she understood why they needed help.

There was an entire pack of werewolves she counted eighteen at least and half as many boggarts. She didn't recognize any of the wolves, but she knew who the boggarts were. They were the same family that was responsible for attacking her mother.

Technically, they were actually Jamie's Aunts and Uncles. Sam was listening to Jamie's thoughts and chimed in, don't worry I can help you take care of them once and for all right now.

Sam swooped low and laid down a wall of fire in the group of werewolves and they scattered. Some of them were a little crispy; some on fire and the others ran just smoking.

Sam circled and made another diving run. This time she grabbed one boggart and bit him in half. She turned her head and chomped another one down.

Jamie jumped off Sam's back and ran to Joe and Jace and said "Sam and I will take care of this bunch, you take your sister and get to the house. She looked around and said "where's Justin and Aundrea?"

Just then a huge Dire Wolf came loping back to the group with Jada and Justin flying just above it.

Jamie looked at them and asked Joe, "Can Jada and Jace ride on one of your backs in your animal form? Joe looked at

Justin and said "Sure, why?" Jamie answered, "Because it might be faster and MaMere's using everything she's got to hold off the storm."

Justin changed into a prehistoric Cave Bear and Jada changed back to her human form. Jada asked Jamie, "I don't see why I had to change, I am faster as my owl and lighter too."

Jamie sighed with impatience and yelled over the howling of the wind, "Because there is a storm from Hell trying to consume the island and you two are so light you would be the first to be sucked up in the wind!

"Dammit do what I told you and haul ass to MaMere's house NOW!" As a unit, they all took off at once.

Jamie turned and found that Sam had either eaten or fried all but 5 of the boggarts and two wolves. Jamie grabbed her crossbow and started firing. She got three boggarts in a row because they were still focused on trying to pin down Sam. The other two realized what was happening and turned to face Jamie. Then the wolves attacked Sam's hindquarters. Jamie was about to fire when Sam turned toward her and chomped both of the boggarts that were about to get to Jamie.

Sam didn't even notice the two werewolves attached to her rear leg. Jamie hitched her chin at Sam pointed to her leg and said "aren't you forgetting something?" Sam looked to her rear and replied "Every time I get around these things the dumb mutts always start humping my leg." She blasted them with a stream of fire and sent them yelping and running for water.

Jamie asked Sam "That was just a short little blast, why didn't you kill them?" Sam said, "The Were's were spelled, couldn't you smell it on them? They will have some nasty burn marks for a few changes but most of them will survive." Jamie said that she couldn't smell or sense anything but would mention it to MaMere as soon as they got back to the house. Maybe it would have some bearing on what was going on and who was behind it. Jamie remounted and they took off for the house.

When they got closer to the house they could see the Hell Storm had now reached the house. MaMere was still working, but you could see the strain she was under.

When they all got inside, she dropped her arms and transported inside. All the windows and doors slammed shut and MaMere was sitting in her chair by the fireplace breathing hard. She was clearly exhausted.

29 DEM DAMN BLOODSUCKERS

Everyone had gathered around her and were waiting for her to speak. When MaMere had caught her breath, she told everyone under no circumstances were they to open the door, window or fireplace flue for anything, no matter what they saw or heard. She told them that the house could not be burned, so even an illusion of fire was no reason to leave the house.

Hawk said "what about water?" MaMere looked at him and said, "I have a special relationship with Poseidon and Calypso and besides that the Nereids are my daughters. Some of de old ones are still around but no longer worshipped, dere powers are mostly elemental, dey are basically in forced retirement, so ta speak. Why da ya tink Ah chose dis place, Chere. This island in Old Lady Lake is well protected by water from creatures of any kind."

"Do you know why they called the storm?" Hawk asked. "Chere, dey is gonna bring dose damn bloodsuckers to my island ta try and turn some a ya'll's minds. As long as we stay in de house and don go outside, dey can't come in. Dat much is true bout de legend of the Nosferatu."

I said "You mean Nosferatu as in vampires?" "Yeah Chere, but vampires dey not dose purty people like is on de TV, non. Dese vampires can make ya one a dem wit jes one bite and a zombie wit a scratch. Dey suck ya blood yeah, but dat ain't de worst part. When dey suck all ya blood, dey also suck out yer soul too, yeah. De blood keeps dere bodies juicy and mobile, but de soul is what keeps dem alive. When dey git strong souls, lahk yours, it lasts a long tahm and makes dem stronger, human souls done las so long."

"So dat's why dey is so hungry fo us. When dey sucks out a soul, dey can also make demselves look lahk de person whose soul de took for a while, so don't go trustin any friends or long lost relatives dat might want to pay us a visit tonight."

"What do they really look like?" I asked. MaMere sighed and said, "Chere, dey is horrible. Dey start out lookin like de humans dey were when dey is firs turned. Den dey start to turn into de creatures dey will become. Dey are parasites and resemble parasitic bugs, dey lose all body hair, and de skin it becomes clear an rubbery so when dey is full they kinda look pink and swollen like a mosquito. De skin will tear like rotted meat if you rub it too hard, but it grows back with more blood. All de body hair and hair on de head stops growin because dey feed only on blood and protein and use all it on fuel for de body. Dey can regenerate dey limbs, but not de head, but if ya don't destroy de head dey can pull it back to dey bodies and rise again."

"Ya can't really kill dem unless you chop off de head and burn it to ashes. Dey won't burst into flames like in the movies, but dey skin does bubble and burn in de sun, but it won't kill dem, it jes makes dem really weak and vulnerable. Dey has fangs yeah, but not doze pearly whites. Dey is drippin wit poison and all de teeth is fangs, kinda lahk snake fangs but a whole mouth full of dem. Dey teet actually siphon de blood, dey done swallow it, no. De teet bring de blood strait to de brain, an from dere to de heart and veins. Dere bites aren't two little holes dat close up. Dey chews at you to get every last drop until dey git to an artery. Left to alone to feed, dey will turn a human into hamburger meat."

I asked "Isn't there a legend that if you kill the Master Vampire, that it will destroy all of them?" MaMere chuckled and said "Jamie, go make me some of my special Tea, Chere. We have a long time till dis storm passes so I might as well tell ya'll de real beginnins of de Nosferatu."

Jamie made the tea and everyone sat around MaMere to listen. MaMere made herself comfortable and sipped her tea. She began; "There a famous poet who got de story almost right. He changed it of course, but de bones of de story are dere if ya know what ya lookin fa."

"De poem he wrote some of you may already know, 'The Rhyme of the Ancient Mariner' by Samuel Hamilton Coleridge, written in the early 1800's. I have it in one

of my books dere on de shelf." She
motioned for Justin to get it for her.

Dan and Hawk both chimed in that they
had read it many times and that there was
a statue in Florida of the Albatross in the
poem.

Justin handed her the book she pointed
to, "Yeah Chere, das de one. Let's see
now, her it is. As the poem goes, there is
a Sea Captain who sets out on a long
voyage in good weather. But soon after
they set out, dey were engulfed in a storm
dat blew dem south for several days until
dey ended up in icy waters and became
stuck in the ice. Dey prayed for release
from their icy hell when an Albatross came
and circled their ship. They fed de great
beast and den the ice began to split and
dey were freed.

The Albatross guided dere ship for
several more days and it circled de ship
begging for food all de while. Irritated with
de constant screeching and flapping of
wings, de Captain Shot de bird. When de
crew rose again de next day, de bird was
nowhere to be found.

"Dat next day a crewmember found dat
birds' body floating in de water. The crew
became suspicious and accused de Captain

of de deed. Then de favorable wind that had guided and protected dem had died done down to nuttin. De currents were still and de ship was in becalmed waters."

"When de food and water ran out, the crew took de body of de Albatross and hung it 'round de Captain's neck in hopes that de bad luck he had caused would belong to him alone. Aahh, here it is" she said reading from the book.

The verse went:

With throats unslaked,
with black lips baked,
We could nor laugh nor wail;
Through utter drought
all dumb we stood!
I bit my arm,
I sucked the blood,
And cried,
A sail! A sail

"Yes, it was a sail all right, a ship or de bones of a ship and de only crew aboard was de Specter o' Death and his mate Lady Life in Death. Dey were throwing lots for the souls of the crew and de Captain."

"Death won the right to de crew, but Lady Life in Death won de Captain. Death awarded the crew an instant merciful death, but Lady Life in Death upon seeing de carcass of de Albatross cursed him to live as he was for all eternity."

"As I said the poem is de bones of de story. De drunken poet listened to my Calypso's sad musings one night and re-created his own version of de story. De story is all correct except for one or two details that she neglected to tell dat poet."

"De details dat were left out were dat de Albatross was actually one of her lovers dat had slighted her in some way, so she turned him into a bird to teach him a lesson. De man dat became the Albatross had been a sailor and so, in his own nature, had protected de ship dat Calypso had been toying wit."

"The foolish Mariner, shot de lover dead thereby incurring Calypso's wrath. Calypso becalmed dat water and stranded de ship and whispered of dc souls about to pass to de Specter and His Lady. Calypso told her story of woe and loss to de Lady and extracted her promise of de eternal curse."

"The eternal curse is to thirst for blood and a soul that would release him to

Heaven or Hell. I have actually met dat Mariner and he is still alive to dis day.

However, he is consumed by de guilt and he struck a bargain with a demon to be released from his curse. De end result, to de demon's delight was dat he was not released unto death, but instead his progeny from dat time forward were distorted into de parasites dey are today."

"He now fights to rid de world of de parasites he helped create. Dere are a few of his children created before the bargain was struck that help perpetuate de parasitic race because dey carry de Mariner's blood. Dey are constantly at war with each other because dey won't agree to stop making more vampires. Some of dem tink dey can take over the world and use de humans like cattle."

"De Mariner's argument is dat if dey keep makin more vampires dey will lose control o' dem and dey will go on a killing rampage and destroy de Human race and ultimately dere own food source. If dere is vampires on dis island, you may meet him before this night is done."

Jamie asked, "But I thought you said we couldn't open the doors for any reason. MaMere sighed and said "Chere, dat man has been in dis house many times, so his welcome in my home still stands. As wit Vampires, what you done know is dat for a demon to enter your home, ya have ta invite him in as well. A demon can't give a power greater dan his own and so a vampire has dat disadvantage too, yeah."

"The details of de bargain were dat if De Mariner completed a task fa de demon den de demon would release him from his curse. He was tasked wit tryin to retrieve a certain wooden cup fa de demon. He failed in his task of course, but he was granted powers by de demon to begin his task to start wit and still carries dem. Doze powers included being able to walk in de sun wit out ill effect, de strength of a demon, de powers of coercion or mind control and de ability to change his shape."

Jamie said, "You still have de cup, how did you stop him from getting it?" MaMere's eyes twinkled and she said "Ah didn't, I gave him de cup, but I tol him what kind of cup it was."

Open mouthed Hawk asked "and then what happened?" "Well, ya see, I could see into de man's heart. He started out bein a good man from de beginning. He was tormented by what de curse dat compelled him ta do tings he had to do to survive confirming he was still a good man. A man dat will go to such lengts ta keep from hurtin good people would never keep a cup dat would release Hell on de Eart if it wound up in de demons' hands."

Dan asked "Do crosses and religious artifacts work on vampires." MaMere said, "The Mariner held the cup in his hands. I don't think you can get more religious than that. Due to the nature of de original curse, dey cannot touch salt or sea water. Which is why I am curious as to why and how dey intend to land on my island?"

30 SOMETHNG WAS ATTACKING OUR ATTACKERS

The storm was raging, it sounded as if it was trying to tear the little house to pieces all by itself. Everyone was nervous and on edge.

MaMere was sitting in her chair with her eyes closed, resting. The others were sitting at the table playing cards and Jamie paced. I took another book off the bookshelf at random and started reading (or just thumbing through the illustrations).

It was some kind of biography with hand-drawn maps, though I couldn't tell you who it was about or where the maps were from lost in thought as I was. I picked it up because of the unusual texture and patina of the outside cover of the book. MaMere gently took it from me and said "Not dat one Chere, it's Jean's Ships Logs."

Suddenly there was a banging and crashing on the sides and windows of the house. That lasted for a few minutes and then came a female voice calling for help from outside the house.

Hawk sat straight up. "Lynne! That's my Lynne!" He made a dash for the front door. MaMere moved faster and was instantly between him and the door. She said, "Robert, Mon Amie, dat isn't Lynne, non. You sent her away two days ago, remember, Chere? Dey is jes using her voice tru yo memories, yeah. Ees a trick, dey have to have ya to open de door Dey cain't jest do it demselves."

Hawk was furious, he turned on MaMere "What if it isn't a trick and they got her before she could get out of town?" MaMere said "Chere, when ya tol me you was sendin her away to her sisters' house, AH also sent a message ta her ta go somewhere else so dey couldn't pick out de location from ya mind. Trust me now, dis is a trick. Dey cain't get into MY head and only Ah know where she and de others are."

As soon as she got the words out of her mouth, the voice changed to my mother's voice. Of course I didn't move, but it was very strange feeling hearing my dead mother's voice calling for help even though I knew it wasn't real. I looked at Jamie and she was obviously under some kind of strain. I reached for her with my mind and found that she was battling some kind of force trying to penetrate her mind.

Instinctively, I poured all my strength into her. She relaxed a little and looked at me. She said that just before they heard Lynne's voice that she felt a presence searching for our minds. She was trying to put up a shield to block it, but there were too many of them and they were bombarding her.

As soon as I gave her my strength, she was able to build a wall to keep them out. The voices had stopped, but the pounding on the house increased. Every few minutes we would hear a high pitched screaming and screeching as if there was something else out there that was attacking our attackers.

I looked at MaMere and said "Is something else out there?" She also had been concentrating on something and said, "Yes, the vampires are here. I have many defenses to this house and island. I have sent my Nereids to attack them with salt water, but they can only go just so far from the water."

"Alan Crowley has finally reached this island and is working to help the Witches he sent here to control and direct the storm. He is a powerful Witch with a very evil bloodline and is very determined to get what he wants."

MaMere took my hand in hers and grabbed Jamie's hand too. As soon as were all linked, there was an explosion of thought. Then I was able to "see" what she was looking at.

She was giving us an aerial view of the island. The storm felt like it was touching me physically and I shuddered. The thought of evil hands grasping at my body and the images that started surfacing in my mind were horrible.

I lost track of what was going on and started to panic and thrash against their hands to get away from it. Then I heard Jamie's voice in my head telling me to be still and concentrate. I felt a calm feeling come to me from MaMere.

The island came into view again. I could still feel the storm grasping at me, but this time I didn't panic.

In the front of the house the beautiful naked, silvery women I had seen come to the island with Jamie were fighting with some of the vampires. They were jumping on them and fighting them with teeth and claws.

When I looked closer I noticed that some of these women had rows of shark teeth. The vampires were fierce and were also fighting with tooth and claw. However, when the vampires touched a Nereid their skin burned and turned black, so they couldn't get a good hold on the women. Hearing my thoughts, Jamie answered my question before I could ask it. "It's the saltwater in their systems."

MaMere pointed out the man called the man called the Mariner. He was fighting off all attackers from the front porch. Somehow he didn't look like what I expected.

When I first looked at him he appeared to be a very tall man in his forties dressed in a plaid shirt and jeans. Then I noticed something odd the longer I watched him.

It was as if the first image of him I saw was super-imposed on another image. The image underneath was of an emaciated creature that looked like a Dachau victim, his skeleton clearly showing beneath his translucent skin.

He was completely bald. He roared when a Troll charged at him and I could see the teeth. MaMere was right. These weren't the pearly whites that have been popularized by television. They were very long like an oversized cobra. Dripping blood and green Troll Gore they were stained black by years of blood.

He was also very quick and was using something that looked like a Japanese Katana and some kind of war axe (he moved them so fast, they were a blur).

As a Troll or a vampire would come hurtling at the front door, he would cut them to ribbons. I knew personally what kind of strength you had to use to cut down a Troll and he made it look like they were made of butter.

The trolls were also throwing things at him like big rocks, trees, anything they could get their hands on. He was so fast, one minute you knew he would get crushed and the next minute he was in another place. I didn't know how long he could keep this up, but I was glad he was on our side.

The whole time I was watching him I kept feeling something pulling at me. Then he looked directly at me and yelled "GO!" Then I realized the thing that was pulling at me was MaMere and Jamie.

MaMere shouted "Stop looking at him, he is using his powers to draw the Trolls to him, you are being sucked in too!"

The Nereids were keeping them from the land in front of the house. There were vampires climbing up onto the roof of the house from the rear. They were trying to tear the house down board by board, shingle by shingle. It was like watching a bowlful of candy stuck in the middle of an anthill.

As I watched, my mind started to grasp that I was one of the pieces of candy being swarmed. Again, MaMere sent me a calming wave. She said, "Watch for the weak spots in their attack Dan. You are a man of strategy, find what you need and use it. Jamie, help him, use your power."

I felt Jamie searching. Our view rose a little higher so that we could see the entire island. On the left side of the island, a large group of men were screaming and charging the vampires and Trolls.

I asked Jamie who they were and when she looked she shook her head in dismay, "Those dear friend are humans, though sometimes I wonder. They are the Cajuns who live in this area."

They were using shotguns and I said "I thought that guns wouldn't kill a vampire?" MaMere answered my question, "Dem crazy Coon Asses have loaded dey guns wit rock salt yeah. Never underestimate a Cajun when yer poachin on his fishing grounds! Aieeee!"

The group of Witches were still where we left them, but there was another man that had joined their ranks. MaMere said it was Alan Crowley. He was helping them focus on something that was connected to the island.

They were using the storm to form some kind of bridge from the mainland to the island and the vampires were using it to cross the brackish waters to get to the island.

Jamie said to focus hard on breaking their link. If we could break the link the bridge would disappear and we would be able to fight them and cut off their stream of reinforcements. I imagined cutting the bridge like cutting a string, but it didn't work.

Jamie said she had an idea. She told MaMere to have some Nereids go to the other end of the bridge and salt it at that end. MaMere looked at her and said "Great idea, but you forget, I am a goddess, I will have the water do the work for us instead."

I asked her how, and she said to just watch. She began to pray. The water began to churn and boil and then it started rising up to the other end. The water rose as a water spout and like a great mouth swallowed the bridge of darkness and kept eating at it like a giant mouth all the way to the island. I asked her why she didn't just use it to melt the vampires on the island.

She said that is where the eye of the storm originates and the power of evil is too strong. Crowley has made some kind of shield to keep the waters from breaking his spell. Near the Swamp, a large party of Trolls were wreaking havoc. Some were being swallowed by the things in the mud pits, but they were still moving enmasse toward the house.

I guess Jean and I missed a couple boatloads of them on the other side of the island or they were like hydras and multiplied when you killed them. I couldn't believe how many of them there were.

Jamie started to get worried. She said a Troll doesn't have to have permission to get into a house they just tear the door down and walk in. MaMere said we needed to get back into our bodies and alert the others to defend the house from the inside.

As our consciousness dropped back to our bodies, I reached for her with my mind and said, "But I thought that you said that you had wards to protect the house and you are a Goddess."

She looked at me a little sadly and said "Yes, I have built wards to protect the house and yes, I am a Goddess, but even I have limits to my powers. I have used up a lot of my power fighting the storm. My powers are as strong as long as water is near, but not unlimited as you may think.

"My dominion is still over the rivers, lakes and streams. My strength in the water is limitless, but on land… not so much, part of the terms of my employment contract, you see."

I asked her "Ok, how do you re-charge?" She said "Normally, I would just walk outside and put my feet in the water. Right now I cannot even open the door. I am not strong enough to hold them back by myself."

I thought about that for a minute and said "So what you are telling me is that you need water to recharge? Kind of like Aquaman?" "I'm not sure who Aquaman is, but yes, I require fresh water to recharge." I said "Forgive me for being blunt, but you do have access to water in the house and a bathtub right?"

While we were standing there looking at each other like idiots, the front door was splintered. Glass shattered in all the windows. The door and storm shutters were holding, but not for long.

Jamie yelled "MaMere go recharge and make it quick, we will hold them off till you are ready!" MaMere ran faster than an old lady should and we grabbed weapons.

Aundrea (whom I discovered was quite a bit bossy) yelled at everyone, "What the hell are you all doing? We're meaner than they are! Let's go kick some ass!"

I guess that was all the motivation we needed, everyone started changing and we all burst out the doors front and back. Hawk, Jace, Aundrea and I took the front and Jamie, Sam and Jada took the back.

Hawk's hands and arms became his talons and he began to shred things as we moved out. The smell of smoke drew his focus to the air and he and Jada joined Sam in their air to ground assault. My swords raised, I felt a surge of power and realized that the power I was feeling was coming from the swords, Cool!

I picked out a vampire who started to charge and began hacking at him. I heard growling and roaring on either side of me, Jace in Cave Bear form and Aundrea as a Dire Wolf were my wing men.

We were a formidable force. Bodies began to stack up all around us. In the melee, I noticed that Jean had also joined us.

I suddenly picked up a stray thought and realized it was Aundrea. She said, "I'm not bossy, I'm assertive, there's a difference! If I hadn't said something you would all have been still standing there with your thumbs up your asses!

Also cool, It didn't occur to me that I could talk to the rest of the Weres with the mind thing.

I guess Jean decided to get in on the conversation (or maybe he was taking the opportunity to bond). He said, "You were almost right the first time, but she's not bossy, she's just Bitchy most of the time. Wait until you get to know them they have been on their best behavior up till now. Most of these humanimals are the most ill-tempered and rude beings you will ever meet and let's not even get into what happens when menses and mating times are in effect.

Aundrea spat back at Jean, "I don't like being called a bitch as a human and I sure as hell don't like being called one as a wolf. You better watch it you overgrown lizard that's a good way to get your head bitten off. At least I was born this way. I'm not the one being punished because I can't control my temper!"

Their banter was felt good to me. My fear washed away and I began to settle in and do some real damage. As much as we were doing, we were just holding our ground, they were still coming. We needed something else.

I called to Jamie and asked her what her situation was. She responded that hers was about the same even with Sam and Hawk. She didn't know how long we could hold them if they continued to send in reinforcements. Then she told me she had an idea, but she would need my help. She needed me to come to her in person. I told the others to cover me so I could get to Jamie and I ran toward the back of the house where she was.

When I finally got there, she pulled me close to her and said that I needed to warn everyone that she was going to start pulling energy and not to fight it. We joined hands like we did with MaMere. I felt the pull as before, but she said she needed more and grabbed me in a bear hug. I held her tightly until I could feel our hearts beating together in unison though our clothes. There was an explosion of thought, emotion and power. Jamie was in my thoughts and I was in hers. This was a new take on the Vulcan Mind Meld.

She chuckled a little at that stray thought and then she told me that while MaMere had used the water to eat up the bridge she had been in her mind and felt the mental push that MaMere had used to do it.

Since then, she kept wondering what Sam meant when she asked her if she was sure she knew she couldn't shift. She said the more she thought about it and it occurred to her that she *was* the child of an Angel *and* a member of the Fae.

She figured that with enough power flowing through her she felt like she could use the same technique and pull enough power to build another shield over the island and drive the invaders out. Almost as an afterthought, she wondered what else she could do.

She told me,"When I start to do my thing, just go with it ok? Do what feels right." Then she started working. She started searching for something. She sent some kind of power feelers out everywhere. Little spikes of energy started tingling through me. I felt like I was a human Leyden Jar Capacitor (static electricity generator).

We were still embracing with our foreheads touching. I made an adjustment and just held her tight and concentrated harder. I believe I knew what she was trying to do, so I relaxed and tried to open up my mind completely.

Once I relaxed and opened up she started pulling energy and pulling hard. I smelled earth and felt the energy and let that flow through me. I felt the wind in my face and the salt spray from the ocean, I felt like I was flying and fed it to her, and I felt a million hearts beating with energy and gave her the pounding rhythm. She amplified all these feelings a thousand fold.

She took all these energies and turned them into light. A light so bright it was like looking into the sun and she focused that light on the Hell Storm. Like someone holding a magnifying glass on a piece of paper the storm started to burn away. The skies started to clear and since it was about three in the afternoon, the sun was still high in the sky.

The vampires on the top of the house started shrieking and running around because their skin was bubbling and burning. The sounds they made came straight from hell. It was a beautiful symphony to me. The wind died down to nothing, but the Trolls were still pounding on the house and kept trying to break in.

MaMere had come from her bath and

joined us. "Good job, Chere. I see you two is starting to use yer heads. Now dat we have de vampires running we can concentrate on getting de Trolls under control."

"How did they get so many of them?" I asked her. She said, "I tol you, Chere, dey have been massing troops for some tahm now. Dey been watching dis ol woman too, yeah. When you showed up dey began movin in."

We followed her down the hall to the others. She ordered Hawk and his flying family to take to the skies, while the rest of us dispersed to clean out the rest of the trespassers.

Before we could so much as take a few steps off the back the porch, a wall of flame was laid down right in front of the porch. We looked up and found that Max was on patrol. Sam who had also joined us laughed and said she should have known he wouldn't stay put.

She ran forward and grabbed a couple of fleeing Trolls, changing mid-stride into her Dragon. As we watched, the struggling Trolls and dying vampires were gobbled up quickly. Hawk joined her. Jace and

Aundrea hit the ground running and changing as well.

Jamie, MaMere and I were still standing on the porch when MaMere said, "You two go for a walk and take care of any stragglers dat de others might miss, although I doubt you will find any….better yet, go find de gurls, Chere. Dey is on dis island somewhere, probably gittin into trouble as usual." Ah will stay here wit Ms. Scratchy Patchy here and survey de damage dese poachers did to my island and put things ta rights.

We started to head out when I nearly tripped on the damned cat that was trying to twine itself around my legs. Apparently Ms. Scratchy Patchy had other ideas about who she wanted to go with. "Awww, she likes you", Jamie giggled. "Go ahead pick her up and give her chin a good rub, she likes that. She doesn't usually prefer anyone other than MaMere, so she must like the way you smell or something."

I hesitated because the cat was so ugly she was sort of cute in a mutant sort of way, but I picked her up and started rubbing her chin. As soon as I heard the purring, my hand started to tingle and then the little cat started to vibrate.

Suddenly, a full grown woman in a dirty, ratty dress reminiscent of Victorian fashion was spilling out of my arms. "What the Hell! the cat is a were-something too?"

I looked at Jamie for an explanation and found that she was staring at me with an open mouth. She threw her hands up and said, "Don't ask me, I have never seen the cat as anything but a cat.

The cat/woman was still purring/humming with her eyes shut and nuzzling her chin on my chest. She had a scarf tied around the wild mess of mousy brown tangles that was her hair.

I gently pushed her off me and asked her if she was ok. She opened her eyes and appeared to be surprised. Then she looked around and patted her head, arms and the rest of her body and started jumping up and down screaming in an old British Cockney accent. "Oy did it, Oy did it, Lordy be, I'm me again. No more bloody fleas for me!"

Then she ran back up to me through her arms around my neck and kissed me full on the mouth.

MaMere came back out of the house to see what the yelling was about and both women started squealing like school girls.

They hugged each other and danced around in circles. "I tol you ya could do it if you just calmed yer nerves, Chere!

"What happened? How did you get yer concentration back?" They walked back up to the porch and the woman sat down in the chairs that just happened to appear where they had been before the war started.

The woman answered. Blimey! "Oy don't know Mum, I noticed what every time dat geezer was 'round, It was easier ter fnk. When they started ter go look fer mawer ov em bleedin invaders, Oy thought ter meself, what Oy wan'ed ter walk wi' 'em an' make sure aahr fngs was still secure, then Oy jist thought 'bouht walkin' wi' 'uman feet an' then da geezer was 'oldin' me, an' I was me bloody self again!

Jamie and I looked at each other with blank looks and then looked at MaMere. "What did she say?"

MaMere bubbling with laughter answered, "She's just a little excited, let me see if I can translate. "She said; (minus the Cajun accent again) I thought to myself that I wanted to walk with them and make sure that our things were still secure, then I just thought about walking with human feet and then the man was holding me and I was myself again."

"Bernice aka Scratchy Patchy is speaking an old Cockney form of English. Ah found her a long time ago, wandering de slums of London during de plague."

"She has apparently been tru some kind dramatic trauma an transformed to her cat form in fear, but was unable ta concentrate and center her spirit long enough to change back to her human self. Ah sense that she has some serious psychological damage that is the cause. Ah have taken care of her since Ah found her."

"She also has a nervous tic about fleas. She imagined dat she was covered in fleas an constantly cleans herself to de point of pulling most of her fur out. De one human eye ting was de result of trying too hard to transform witout success. She is an excellent organizer though and Ah have deemed her my personal secretary. She keeps track of everything on dis island with acute precision."

"I have lived a very long time and sometimes it is a lot to remember all the details. She helps me a great deal, although I have found that you have to be precise when you ask her to locate something because she uses an organization system that is unique to how she sees things."

Jamie said, "The island isn't that big, how hard could it be?" MaMere's eyes twinkled again and she said "Chere, you is only seeing the top of dis island. It is much bigger dan you tink, yeah."

While were talking to MaMere, I was watching Bernice mumble and hum to herself, pick knots out of her tangled hair and examine her own hands as if she was amazed how they worked. It appeared to me that the woman was exactly as she appeared, a neurotic mess. I wondered if she heard voices too.

MaMere turned to Bernice and asked her, "Bernice, can you locate Maddey and Adey?" Bernice just continued to mumble and examine her hand. MaMere asked again, "Bernice can you locate any children on this island?" Still no answer.

She asked again, "Bernice, can you locate the Balance of Magic on this island?" Bernice blinked, the connection to what MaMere was asking her finally registering to her, she said "Blimey! Coarse I can! They're in da bloody swamp wiv da bleedin Fairies an' dat Man-Witch bloke."

31 IT IS YOU WHO ARE MISTAKEN

MaMere jumped and yelled, "Hang on, Alan Crowley has found them! We've got to get to them!" She grabbed us by the front our clothes and zapped us all to the Swamp.

As Bernice said, Alan Crowley was in the swamp with some other Witches and some kind of small leprechaun looking creatures. They were obviously looking for something.

As soon as we popped in, the man that I assumed was Crowley threw up some kind of bubble that covered the group entirely.

He looked a bit ridiculous if you ask me. I guess it might impress females, but I thought his getup made him just look like he had read too many of those bodice ripper romance novels. He was wearing skin tight leather pants with a large silver belt buckle, thigh high, high healed boots, a black heavily embroidered vest with no shirt, pulllease! And to top it off, he was wearing a full cape with a high collar!

I was beginning to wonder which side his sexual preferences were on when he confirmed my suspicions by tossing his long stringy blonde hair like a wanna be rock star from the eighties.

MaMere stood armed with her staff, Jamie had been outfitted with her crossbow and I suddenly had my swords in hand. I looked down at a movement at my feet and saw that Bernice was the weird cat again complete with mismatched eyes.

The little cat had all the remaining fur on her back standing straight up. Her back was arched, teeth bared, doing a weird sideways dance, hissing and spitting for all she was worth.

MaMere addressed the Witch (or was it Warlock?), "Mr. Crowley, Ah believe you are trespassing on my land, Chere. Ah hate to be an ungracious host, but Ahm gonna have to ask you to leave, yeah."

Alan Crowley answered her, "My dear Mrs. Eschte, I know you have the Balance on this little mud bog you call home. If you will just relinquish it to me, no one else will get hurt."

MaMere looked daggers at him and her tone was earily calm, "Why Mr. Crowley, no one who belongs here has been hurt, I believe you are mistaken."

He crowed back at her, "No Ma'am, You are the one who is mistaken." He pointed to the ground at his feet and the other witches (who apparently had the same stylist and were wearing capes as well) moved aside so we could see what they were concealing.

Hawk and Joe were lying on the ground in their animal form, covered in something that looked like black tar. They were both very still.

MaMere, never blinked an eye. She simply raised her cane and a bolt of energy shot forward and blasted the bubble they were encased in… Nothing happened.

Crowley howled in triumph. "I knew it! I am finally stronger than you! Old Lady, you have finally met your match!"

MaMere's eyes shined (no twinkle this time) and she asked him, "What you done

Chere? How did you get so strong all of a sudden?" Obviously he had never seen any old Batman episodes. Doesn't he know that while the bad guy is gloating, the good guys are getting free? Sure enough, I looked at Hawk and his eyes were open and they both started moving slightly.

Crowley, getting bolder, stepped in front of his captives lying on the ground and closer to the edge of his bubble, "When I saw that you were about to ruin my storm bridge, I re-channeled the energy into myself! I now have all the power of the Hell Storm inside me! You have been a constant thorn in my side for a hundred years you old biddy! Now I am going to destroy you once and for all!"

MaMere said, "What'cha gonna go an do something like dat for, Chere? Ah'm jest an old woman who ain't never hurt you, Mais non."

Crowley sneered, "Is that so? Every time my Cabal gets close to doing anything near this place, it goes wrong. I am done with your meddling old woman and with you out of the picture all my plans will come together nicely."

MaMere continued in her polite demeanor, "What makes you tink you is stronger dan me Chere?" Crowley laughed again, "Are you kidding, you couldn't even blast my circle away! My power is too strong!" MaMere extended her hand, palm up and said innocently, "Chere, I wasn't trying to blast your circle, I was making it mine."

Crowley, obviously stunned, took another step forward and tried to step out of the bubble. He was stopped cold. He shouted, "Impossible!" He raised his arms in the air and started chanting and sweating.

MaMere looked down and addressed Hawk and Joe, "Finish yer change boys and come on out to dis side, so Ah can clean dis mess up"

Hawk and Joe did as she asked, but as Joe started to step through the bubble, one of the witches grabbed hold of Joe's arm and tried to step through with him. The witches' hand on Joe's arm burst into flame and sent the witch screaming back into the bubble.

Crowley began to realize his predicament and put his hands to his temples and concentrate harder. I guess he was trying to call for help, because I heard a distinct buzzing in my head for a moment and then it was gone.

He sank to his knees defeated; "This is not possible, you don't have that much power, you are just a meddling old swamp witch. Who is helping you?"

MaMere looked at him with pity, "Alan Chere, you are a LeFey. Yer great-great-grandmother was jest like you, yeah. Always wantin something she didn't earn. She was corrupted by evil Chere. You cannot love someone who is evil. She was jealous of the joy others in found love. In her greed and thirst for power, she decided she wanted to able to control the power that love gives. She tried to force others to love her to achieve dat power, but she didn't realize dat to get love you have to make de compromises and sacrifices dat love requires. Love is the opposite of evil and in dat there is no compromise."

"Nuttin in dis life is easy an you LeFey's have always been a lazy bunch, you...lookin for powers you cannot control that would force others to give you what you wanted. Dat's when you start messin in tings dat you have no business in, non."

Crowley whined, "What are you talking about, Morgana was the most powerful sorceress of all time! She defeated Merlin! Her bloodline was passed down from generation to generation to me!

I have her spells and with the new power raging inside me I will be even greater than she was! I have also taken measures and refused to be corrupted by the need to acquire love as she was! Love is weak. My new alliances have shown me a way to get power, pure power without morality, judgement or self sacrifice."

MaMere just shook her head, "No, she was pure evil and so are you. An dats why you will always fail, Chere. You are right 'bout me havin help, but it's not de help ya tink. Chere, my power comes from openin my heart and prayin to de only real power dat matters… I pray to God and He gives me de strength I need to do what is right, Mais yeah."

Crowley pounded the ground with his fists, "I can't believe this! I am being held by an old Swamp Witch turned Holy Roller! You're lying!" MaMere stared at him for a minute and then she said, "Den you are going ta need a stronger lesson 'bout meddling in tings you know nuttin about, foolish mortal."

She started to give off a shimmering glow and she grew and grew and grew until she was as more than twenty or so feet tall. She became Tethys.

"I am no Swamp Witch you fool. The power you ingested is corrupting your mind, body and soul. The only hope you have now is that Yahweh will understand and forgive your ignorance and greed... for now, you will die."

She raised one hand and looked toward the sky and pointed the finger of her other hand and fried him with a lightning bolt. Just like Lot's wife, he turned to salt and crumbled before our eyes. When we turned to look back at Tethys, she was MaMere again and the girls were at her side. Jamie ran to embrace them and asked them where they had been.

32 DE GNOMES KNOW

The girls both looked at her and giggled and said "We were right here!" Then they both disappeared and then reappeared. How did you do that? Jamie asked. Maddey, the leader, shuffled her feet and said, "Well, while Max was sleeping, we sort of listened in on his dreams".

Adey interrupted her and said one word, "Camouflage." Maddey gave her an exasperated look and said," ANYWAY, (rolling her eyes) We learned how to do all sorts of things! Do you know that Sam and Max keep getting born over and over again?"

Adey piped in "Reincarnated." Jamie looked at both of them and then at

MaMere, "Well, that explains how they know about things not of their time. We need to get these two back to the house and have a long talk." Jamie and the others began making their way back to the house.

I asked MaMere, "What are you going to do with the rest of them?" She shrugged, "Nuttin, Chere. Dey is free ta go."

The Witches having heard us talking turned and started running toward the shoreline with Scratchy Patchy hot on their heels. When Scratchy caught them she was going to teach them what it meant to be a "Witches Familiar." Although she was small, she moved lightning fast and she was like a little buzz-saw with those razor sharp claws of hers. I wouldn't want to have her mad at me, she would skin me alive ... literally.

The little creatures that I had noticed were still standing there watching MaMere. They were a little more than two feet tall and were dressed rather primitively with a loin cloth that resembled the type that early American Indians wore in the movies. (They bring to mind the little dolls that people used to put on the dash of their cars with the wild fuzzy hair with smaller facial features) They also had leather belts with little pouches attached on some of them. As I looked at them more closely, I began noticing other strange details.

They had a fine covering of hair all over their bodies that was almost transparent and while I counted several males, there was only one female present and judging by her size compared to the others, she appeared to be a prepubescent of their race.

She saw me looking at her and gave me a little smile filled with tiny needle-like teeth. They had smallish eyes, noses that sort of melted into their faces and a light brown muddy skin tone. Intrigued, I looked further and noticed that they wore no shoes but had six toes on each foot but only four fingers on their hands. Incredibly, I realized they resembled moles.

"Why aren't they leaving?" I asked. She said, "Because dey are Gnomes and dey live here." Confused, I asked "What were they doing with the Witches?" She said, "Dem Witches had dem spelled. Dey was tryin to use dem to find my treasures they taut was buried here."

"Why would the Gnomes know? I thought that was the Cat's job." I asked. She said "A Gnome is a creature dat's in tune wit de Eart. Anyting that's involves their realm, de know about it."

Still confused, I said, "Then, shouldn't they have been able to find your stuff?" "No Chere, dey couldn't, because on dis island, de Gnomes know what's here, dey just can't "remember" where. It was one of the little safeguards I gave dem when dey moved in. Dey maintain the bogs and other security traps for me and I give dem a place dey can live out dey lives without having to hide from humans. Dey is simple creatures, but dey size and eating habits are a little hard to hide from humans."

We began the long walk back to the house with the children and Jamie running ahead of us. I asked MaMere, "is the danger over?" She looked thoughtful for a moment and said, "I dunno, Chere. I still feel like something is wrong and I can't put my finger on it. De Trolls have been chased away by Sam and Max, the Were's have been released from de spell dey was under when I killed Mr. Crowley, but I still feel uneasy, like there is something else coming dat is worse dan everything else so far."

We walked in silence for a while longer and when she asked me "You ok, Chere? It must bother you that you have seen a lot of death these couple of days." I thought about it and truthfully, I think that I was still in shock.

I felt like everything that I once knew and thought was important was only a daydream. I felt guilty because I didn't feel bad about killing those Trolls or seeing a Human get killed.

With another twinkle in her eye, she told me, "By de way, Chere, ya might wanna take special care wit de cleaning and care of dose swords. Ya need to keep dem wit ya at all times, yeah."

Suspicious, I asked her what she meant by that. She looked ahead to make sure that Jamie and the others wouldn't over hear her and she told me in what I now call her Tethys Speak, "These are the swords of my dear friend Perseus.

"They served him well back then. They have been imbued with the power of the Gods. They have not served mankind since the time of Perseus because there has not been a human worthy of them until now.

Bernice has a talent and insight much deeper than I gave her credit for. She saw something in you that gave the Swords of Perseus a reason to serve mankind once again."

"Poor girl, I hope that she may eventually be healed from whatever traumatized her so much. Although she has made progress with you here, much more than I was ever able help her achieve. You are indeed more special than even I realized."

I told her that had I felt a rush of power when I used them and wondered where it came from. She just nodded in understanding.

I asked her what we were going to do with all the bodies. She said that they would burn the vampires that Sam and Max missed and between the Cajuns and the Gnomes, they would take care of the rest.

Somehow even though I was still trying to get my "Sea Legs" with all this, it finally felt right. I didn't feel outcast or like an oddity of nature anymore. Hell, even in the bright sunlight my eyesight now seemed to have been healed. It was as if when I opened my mind to be able to "see", my eyes weren't carrying all the burden of filtering what was being sent to me. I felt free for the first time in my life.

I started to answer her question and then changed to sending her my feelings instead. She continued our conversation in the same fashion. She said "So now ya know who and what we are, Chere. Now you have de task of takin care of tellin our story to da world in a way dat will not bring us more troubles.

With all that had happened in the past couple of days, I had completely forgotten about why I had even come here in the first place. I had a feeling that she knew that there was no way I could reveal their secrets. Oh wait; correction... OUR secrets. It finally sank in that I was a part of this world and its unusual inhabitants.

33 PROLOGUE

News article – Sun Tribune –
June 12, 2012
Headline –
Heirs to Hamilton Fortune Found!

Investigations have concluded that Mrs. Marie Eschte Hamilton gave birth to a daughter, Dr. Jamie Eschte Delahousse on March 2, 1943 at Terrebonne General Hospital in Houma, Louisiana. Mrs. Delahousse has produced birth certificates that validate her birth.

It was later discovered that Mrs. Delahousse had been raised by her maternal Grandmother, Mrs. Estelle Eschte of Old Lady Lake, Louisiana.

Unfortunately, the child's birth was the result of the violent crime of statutory rape for Mrs. Hamilton when she was a teen. Mrs. Hamilton simply couldn't bear the trauma of the situation and gave custody to her grandmother at the time.

While the Niece and Nephew of Mr. Hamilton are still contesting the will, Mrs. Delahousse has concurred with her Mother's wishes and has agreed not to contest the will as it stands. The entire value of the Hamilton Estate approximated to be worth in excess of two hundred million dollars will be donated to the Our Lady of the Lake School.

Dr. Delahousse currently lives in New Zealand doing charitable research with infant mortality rates. Her husband Barry Delahousse was critically injured in an oil field accident and perished many years ago. The couple had two children, both girls (names will not be disclosed at the family's request for privacy).

Due to allegations from Mr. Hamilton's Niece and Nephew, the Our Lady of the Lake Foundation was also investigated. While the school was designed for Special Children as is stated in their charter, it is a private school, privately funded and maintained and is designed to nurture children of special talents and abilities such as art, music, writing, athletics and so forth, it also encourages children with special intuitive abilities, which is a small part of their curriculum.

The charter was designed to encourage children with ANY ability without discrimination. As a result, the school also has a very successful program that provides unique instruction techniques for the mentally handicapped.

By Dan Rawlings – Freelance Investigative Journalist and Public Relations Coordinator for Our Lady of the Lake Foundation.

34 CHARACTERS –HISTORICAL AND LITERARY REFERENCES

The Mariner – a fictional character created by this author and inspired by the poem written by Samuel Taylor Coleridge, The Rime of the Ancient Mariner.

The Rime of the Ancient Mariner (originally The Rime of the Ancyent Marinere) is the longest major poem by the English poet Samuel Taylor Coleridge, written in 1797–98 and published in 1798 in the first edition of Lyrical Ballads.

Tethys - Daughter of Uranus and Gaia was an archaic Titaness and aquatic sea goddess, invoked in classical Greek poetry

but not venerated in cult. Tethys was both
sister and wife of Oceanus. She was
mother of the chief rivers of the world
known to the Greeks, such as the Nile, the
Alpheus, the Maeander, and about three
thousand daughters called the Oceanids.

Considered as an embodiment of the
waters of the world she also may be seen
as a counterpart of Thalassa, the
embodiment of the sea. Tethys meaning
"grandmother", and she is often portrayed
as being extremely ancient

Arachnia – a character invented by this
author.

Jean Lafitte -(ca. 1776 – ca. 1823) was a
pirate and privateer in the Gulf of Mexico in
the early 19th century.

Lafitte is believed to have been born
either in France or the French colony of
Saint-Domingue. By 1805, he operated a
warehouse in New Orleans to help disperse
the goods smuggled by his brother Pierre
Lafitte. After the United States government
passed the Embargo Act of 1807, the
Lafitte's moved their operations to an
island in Barataria Bay. By 1810, their new
port was very successful; the Lafittes

pursued a successful smuggling operation and also started to engage in piracy.

Though Lafitte tried to warn Barataria of a British attack, the American authorities successfully invaded in 1814 and captured most of Lafitte's fleet. In return for a pardon, Lafitte helped General Andrew Jackson defend New Orleans against the British in 1815.

Lafitte continued pirating around Central American ports until he died trying to capture Spanish vessels in 1823. Speculation around his death and life continue amongst historians.

Nereids – In Greek mythology and, later, Roman mythology, the Oceanids were the three thousand daughters of the Titans Oceanus and Tethys. Some of them were closely associated with the Titan gods (such as Calypso, Clymene, Asia, Electra) or personified abstract concepts.
One of these many daughters was also said to have been the consort of the god Poseidon typically named as Amphitrite. More often, however, she is called a Nereid

Oceanus and Tethys also had 3,000 sons, the river-gods Potamoi ("rivers"). Whereas most sources limit the term Oceanids or Oceanides to the daughters, others include both the sons and daughters under this term.

Characters in this book are all fictitious. Any similarity to actual persons, places or events is pure coincidence.

35 GLOSSARY OF TERMS AND PRONOUNCIATIONS

MaMere – pronounced MaMeh, Cajun French slang term for Grandmother

Chere – In Louisiana Cajun French it is pronounced SHA and means Dear, often used in conversation as an endearment.

Court-bouillon – Pronounced Koo Bee Yawh, an old French word meaning the Kings Soup.

Ammolite – from fossilized Ammonites the Gemstone has an iridescent opal-like play of color mostly in shades of green and red;

all the spectral colors are possible,
however.

Mais Non or Mais Yes (or used just as non
or yeah)– Pronounced May No, May Yeah.
In Cajun French the term is often used to
reiterate the positive or negative of the
statement.

Dan – than
Das – that's
De – The
Dey – They
Fo - For
Ya – You
Yer – Your
Don' – don't
Lahk – Like
Dem – Them
Chirren – Children
Chil – pronounced chile meaning child
Demselves – themselves
Ya sef - yourself
Las – last
Tryin – trying
Tahm – time
Purty – pretty
Tol – told
Bein – being

Lengts – lengths
Hurtin – hurting
Ta – to
Eart – Earth
Dat – that
Fa – for
Wit – with
Teet – teeth
Beginnins – beginnings
Drippin – dripping
Gittin – getting
Jes – just
Delahousse – De La Hoosee
Eschte – Esh tayFontenot – Fon ten 0
Benoit – Ben wah
Bauchan – Baw kan
Robicheaux – Row bee show
Thibodeaux – TIB O DOH.

ABOUT THE AUTHOR

This is Sonia Brock's first book (She asks that you please be patient with book formatting). She grew up in Southern Louisiana with her Grandparents and her sister Jamie. The two were inseparable most of their lives and shared many adventures with their Grandmother.

Sonia went to High School in the small town of Rayne, Louisiana. After graduating early, she joined the United States Marine Corps and for a time was separated from her sister.

Sonia married and had two children, the youngest with Down Syndrome. Shortly after her youngest daughter's birth the two sisters reunited and were as close as ever. Fighting and laughing together through thick and thin.

Sonia divorced and shortly after her sister Jamie was killed by a hit and run driver during the proceedings of their Mother's funeral.

In her loss, she met another man who finally understood her. Now, happily married he has encouraged her to fulfill her dreams and write her stories.

Made in the USA
Charleston, SC
26 February 2013